A DAUGHTER'S QUEST

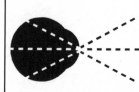

This Large Print Book carries the
Seal of Approval of N.A.V.H.

WILD PRAIRIE ROSES, BOOK ONE

A DAUGHTER'S QUEST

LENA NELSON DOOLEY

THORNDIKE PRESS
A part of Gale, Cengage Learning

GALE
CENGAGE Learning™

Detroit • New York • San Francisco • New Haven, Conn • Waterville, Maine • London

GALE
CENGAGE Learning™

LIBRARY OF CONGRESS CATALOGING-IN-PUBLICATION DATA

Dooley, Lena Nelson.
    A daughter's quest / by Lena Nelson Dooley. — Large print ed.
        p. cm. — (Thorndike Press large print Christian romance)
    (Wild prairie roses; bk. 1)
    ISBN-13: 978-1-4104-2441-9 (alk. paper)
    ISBN-10: 1-4104-2441-3 (alk. paper)
    1. Large type books. I. Title.
PS3554.O5675D38 2010
813'.54—dc22   2009046755

Published in 2010 by arrangement with Barbour Publishing, Inc.

Printed in the United States of America
1 2 3 4 5 6 7 14 13 12 11 10

To our wonderful God and to Gateway Church in Southlake, Texas, where He has planted James and me for this season in our life. Lord, You are doing an awesome thing, and Your vision is so far beyond our reach. Thank You for letting us be a part of the miracle You are performing in this place.

Every book I write is also dedicated to my precious husband, James Allen Dooley. You are always there for me. You love me, cherish me, protect me, and make me laugh. These last forty-two years have been an amazing ride. I never want to get off.

PROLOGUE

April 1867

Dawn sent fingers of sunlight between the Ozark Mountain peaks, bathing Constance Miller in warmth she needed on this early spring morning. She stood near a window, gazing out at the pastel colors spread across the sky by the rising sun, and thanked God for the beauty around her.

Raspy breaths across the room behind her broke the stillness and drowned out the first twitters of birds awakening to the new morning. How she hated the sound that meant her father's death could be imminent.

When the doctor had left yesterday, he had held out no hope for recovery. Without her father's strong presence in her life, Constance's future looked bleak. She couldn't farm this land by herself, and there wasn't a man on the mountain, or even in the valley below, who she would consider marrying. Where did that leave her?

Other young women had ventured far from their Arkansas mountain homes, but she felt no yearning to move away from here. Her gaze was drawn to the golden tint now rimming the tall budding trees, some with tender green leaves, that surrounded their home place. Spring was her favorite time of the year. It usually made her think of a new beginning. But the wheezing gasps coming from the man in the bed on the other side of the room signaled an ending instead. She clasped her arms tight across her chest and shivered in her flannel night-dress.

"Connie." Her father's rasping voice was hardly distinguishable. "Come here, gurl." The last word faded into nothingness.

She whirled and rushed to kneel at the side of the wooden platform covered with a ticking filled with dry corn husks. "I'm here." She removed the rag, which now felt hot, and dipped it into the cold water in the basin on the floor before replacing it on her father's brow.

His bony arm snaked out from under the covers, and his hand gripped her forearm with amazing strength. "You hafta promise me somethin'." His gaze bored into hers, and a fire of determination burned in his eyes.

"Anything, Pa." She wanted to keep him calm. Too much excitement could leach his waning strength too quickly.

"I ain't got much time." He stopped to take another noisy gulp of air. "You gotta listen real good."

Constance nodded and leaned closer to him so he wouldn't have to try to talk so loud.

"I done something real bad when I was gone."

She knew that war was ugly with men killing each other and all, but she didn't think he was talking about that aspect of the war. Surely her pa hadn't done much else. When she started to tell him that, he interrupted her.

"I come up with a plan to steal some gold from those Yankees. It was only Jim Mitchell and me who talked about it, but the next day, I knew God didn't want me to do it." His hold on her arm slackened. "The war made me lose my way for a bit." His hand dropped to lie motionless on the tattered quilt that covered his emaciated body.

She grasped her father's hand. "I knew you couldn't have done anything too bad, Pa."

His eyes fluttered open. "But someone did steal the gold, and they did it jist the way I planned. It had to be Jim." Once again his speech faltered, and his eyelids closed.

Constance moved her head closer to him once again and was thankful that the morning sun began to take the chill from the room as its rays crept across the rough wooden floorboards. "If you didn't do it, then you're not guilty of anything."

Her father opened his eyes again. They held a sadness that went straight to her heart.

"I'm guilty of two things. I hadn't oughta come up with the plan, and I never took the time to tell Jim about God." Once again he relaxed with his eyes closed.

"We all make mistakes, Pa."

"Not like these." He kept his eyes closed as he continued. "I cain't go to my rest unless you make me a promise."

Constance didn't know what she could do about any of this, but she didn't want her father fretting. "I'll promise you anything you want."

Once again, his watery eyes opened, and he stared at her face as if memorizing every inch of it. "Connie, gurl, you gotta go to Iowy and find Jim Mitchell. You gotta tell him about Jesus, then convince him to give back the gold."

She couldn't keep from showing her surprise. "I can't do that. The only time I've ever left this mountain was when I went to school, and that was only in the next valley. I don't even know where Iowa is."

"You gotta find out. Get that schoolmarm to help you . . . or the new preacher, but you gotta go. I won't rest easy unless you promise."

Constance stood and walked over to the table where the wash basin sat beside a bucket of water. She picked up the tin dipper and took a drink, noticing that the container was almost empty. That would mean a trip to the clear stream that ran down the mountain a few yards from the house. She dreaded leaving her father for even the few minutes that would take.

How could she make her father a promise like that? Uncertainty and fear crowded her thoughts.

His breathing became more labored and echoed in the stillness. He wasn't long for this world. *Oh, God, what am I supposed to do?*

A loud snort was followed by her father calling her name again. She rushed over and fell to her knees on the floor, not even being careful about splinters this time.

"I'm here."

A faint smile lit his face for a fleeting moment. "You look jist like your ma." Then his eyes slid closed again, but he continued to speak softly. "If you stand at the window on the west wall of the cabin and count to the seventh board on the floor, you'll find my stash of money."

Constance's gaze went to the wall, and she counted over to where he was talking about. It looked like the rest of the unpainted floor.

"Where the boards come together, the one to the south ain't nailed down. Pick it up, and you'll find the money I've been saving. I meant to go find Jim m'self, but the good Lord had other plans. Jim wrote down the name of the town where his family lives on a piece of paper, and I kept it all this time. It's with the money."

All his energy must have been spent, because he went so slack that Constance thought he might have died right then. She laid her hand on his chest and felt the faint beating of his heart. Tears slipped down her cheeks, and she swiped at them with the backs of her hands. More took their place. She watched him sleep for a few moments before she went over to the board. Constance lifted it and saw a large rusty tin can with a rag tied on the top. She picked it up and took it to the table. After untying the dirty string and lifting the scrap of cloth, Constance's eyes widened at the large roll of paper money stuffed in the can.

She and her father had always had enough to eat and clothes to wear, but that amount of money would have made a difference in their life. Her father wouldn't have had to work so hard, and they could have had a few more nice things. Why had he let his guilty feelings rob them of a better life?

ONE

Hans looked at the words he had painted on a new board: *Van de Kieft Smithy.* Today, he would hang it right after the stagecoach delivered his new anvil. Finally, he was a business owner. He'd worked hard as an apprentice for Homer and then continued working for him several more years before the blacksmith decided to retire on the farm he had bought about five miles from town. Of course, Homer planned to do all his own smithy work, so he wanted to keep his own anvil.

The afternoon stage wouldn't arrive for a while. Hans might as well go ahead and hang the sign while he waited. He picked up several nails and stuck them in his shirt pocket. He shoved the head of the hammer into one of his hip pockets before picking up the sign. After standing in the street in front of the blacksmith shop for a few minutes, looking at the building, he decided to nail it up over the top of the large doorway. He set the sign against the side of the building and went inside looking for his ladder.

Hans wasn't excited about climbing on the thing. He never had liked heights. When the boys played in the hayloft while he was growing up, he tried to stay on the ground as much as possible. He closed the doors and latched them together before he leaned the ladder against them. After testing to see if the ladder was stable, Hans took a tentative step up. Another followed. How many rungs would he need to climb before he could reach far enough to attach the sign?

Good thing he was over six feet tall, so he could reach pretty high. He stepped down and decided to climb back up only four rungs. After hefting the sign over his shoulder, he took a firm grip with his other hand on the ladder. This time, his steps were slower. Finally, he felt secure, but he decided not to look down.

About the time Hans had the sign placed exactly where he wanted it, the ladder swayed. Cold sweat broke out on his forehead, and a voice came from behind and below.

"I'll hold the ladder for you, Hans, while you pound in those nails."

"Thanks, Sheriff." Hans didn't dare look at his friend but was glad he had come by. "I appreciate it."

He quickly pounded nails into the four corners of the sign and stepped back down the ladder. When he was standing safely on solid ground, he thrust out his hand toward the sheriff.

Andrew Morton shook it, then turned to look up at the sign. "It looks nice. You did a good job on the lettering."

"Mother made all of us learn good penmanship, even the boys. I'm glad now." Hans stood in the middle of the street with his hands on his hips to get the full effect. "Everyone should be able to see the sign most anywhere on the street."

He rubbed his hands down the legs of his denim trousers. "I'm going to leave the door closed. Isn't it about time for the stagecoach to arrive? My anvil should be on it today."

Hans started toward the station, and Andrew walked beside him. "I think I'll mosey that direction, too."

Constance glanced around the crowded stagecoach, trying not to show her distaste. The trip had been way too long and much too hard. Some of the people who shared the space with her didn't understand the importance of cleanliness. She could hardly wait to arrive at Browning City, Iowa. When she stepped out of this conveyance, she planned to breathe in a lot of clean, fresh air.

She pressed her hand down the length of dark green gabardine that covered her lap. When Constance had donned the traveling suit in Fort Smith, it had been the most beautiful outfit she had ever owned. She felt sure she didn't need to be ashamed of the way she looked.

Layers of dust almost obliterated the color of the fabric. Several times she had been given the choice of whether to spend the night at way stations and catch the next coach or continue on this one when the fresh horses were harnessed to it. Because of her eagerness to take care of her final promise to her father, she always chose to go on. Now she regretted it. The driver had told them that the next stop was Browning City, and she would arrive dirty with her traveling clothes completely wilted. Why was she always so impetuous? Mother had often warned her to take longer to make decisions. Why hadn't Constance listened?

The grizzled man who sat in the opposite corner of the coach leaned his head out the window and looked in the direction they were going before pulling back into the cabin. "I can see the edge of town up ahead. How many of us are stopping here?"

When Constance was the only one who lifted her hand, he smiled at her.

"I've got a brother who lives several miles west of Browning City. I'll be getting off, too."

Constance glanced out the window in time to see several boys running alongside the vehicle as it began to slow down. A puppy romped around their legs. The houses on her side of the street looked inviting, each wearing a coat of whitewash or paint. None of those unpainted gray cabins such as hers back home in the Ozarks. Some houses had picket fences, while iron railings corralled other yards. This looked like a nice town. Too bad she was only here for one reason.

When the driver stopped the coach in front of the station, Constance noticed two men standing on the boardwalk, eyeing the people in the windows of the coach.

A tall, broad-shouldered man with blond hair long enough to touch his collar turned to his companion. "My anvil is probably in the boot. I'm sure no one wanted to lift it onto the luggage rack on the top." He stepped off into the street.

The driver opened the door. "This is your stop, Miss. I'll get your carpetbag down for you." He stepped up on the front wheel of the coach to reach it.

Constance gathered her reticule and stood up as well as she could in the confines of the coach. She had been sitting so long that her legs felt stiff. She planned on taking a long walk after she checked into a hotel or boardinghouse. Exercise would work the soreness out.

When she reached her foot down for the step, somehow she missed it. She realized that she would land on her face in the dirt. Just what she needed for her entrance into a new town. Constance grabbed onto the handle of the door, but it swung wider, taking her with it. After shutting her eyes, she took a deep breath, preparing for her inglorious landing in the street.

Instead, strong arms lifted her up and away from the coach. Her eyes flew open, and she peered into a handsome face with eyes the color of the sky above.

Without thinking, Hans reached for the woman to stop her from hurting herself. When he lifted her, she felt like a feather in spite of all the layers of skirts that swirled around them. The green hat that matched

20

her clothes was knocked askew and fell over one side of her forehead, almost covering one eye. Her arms clutched him around his neck as she opened her eyes and stared at him.

Everything around them disappeared. When Hans stared into her eyes, they flashed green and brown all at the same time. Golden flecks glistened in the bright sunlight. Fear, surprise, and a questioning look followed each other across her face, leaving her with a vulnerable expression.

Heat suffused his arms and every part of his body that touched her. His stomach began a strange dance that it had never done before, and then it turned over and knotted up. Hans had experienced reactions to young women before, but he had always been able to control them. This felt different — more personal and . . . somehow strange.

Some of the young woman's abundant brown hair fell out of the bun she wore low on her neck. Her cheeks turned red, and her rosy lips parted slightly. His mouth went dry, and Hans tried to swallow, never taking his gaze from her face. The most beautiful face he had ever seen.

As Andrew walked past Hans, he leaned close and whispered for his ears alone, "You can put her down now."

How long had Hans been holding her? He didn't want to look around because he was afraid of what other people might see on his face. Never had he experienced anything quite this intense. It was uncomfortable, yet special somehow. Nothing in his life had prepared him for this moment.

Hans whirled and carefully made his way to the boardwalk. He gently set the woman on her feet and turned back toward the coach. He needed to get his anvil and hurry to his place of business.

"Thank you." Her soft words followed him, but he didn't turn around.

He only hoped she was not staying in town long. He wasn't ready to confront these strange feelings, and he surely didn't want to make a fool of himself.

Two

From the warmth she felt in her cheeks, Constance knew they must contain a blush that hadn't gone away. With her carpetbag sitting at her feet on the boardwalk, she glanced up and down the dusty street. Thankfully, a hotel was on the opposite side, down a ways. After the stage pulled off, she picked up her baggage and started toward the building. She kept her head down and only peeked around, hoping no one noticed what had happened.

As she took her first steps, some of the people standing around followed her with their stares. Even when she was in school, Constance hadn't liked being the center of attention. Her feelings of discomfort welled up and almost overwhelmed her. She wished she had never come so far from home and familiar things. If only her father hadn't asked her to make that promise. She couldn't break a deathbed promise, could she?

When she once again glanced around, the other people on the street were going about their own business as if they had forgotten her. Maybe her inglorious descent from the stage wouldn't haunt her for long.

The tall, handsome blond man who had rescued her strode down the street carrying a heavy anvil as if it didn't weigh much. When he had caught her as she exited the stagecoach, she felt the strength of those bulging muscles. The blacksmith in the mountain community near her home was an old man. Even though he was strong, he never could have had a physique like this smithy.

Constance started down into the street, almost missing the wooden step . . . again. She had to forget that man and pay attention to what she was doing. With as much aplomb as she could manage, she swept toward the hotel. She didn't want anyone to know how out of her element she felt.

Thankfully, the clerk at the hotel didn't seem to know what had happened. Her embarrassment had been on the other side of the coach from this building. He probably hadn't seen her descent and the aftermath, and apparently word of the event hadn't reached him.

"Are you alone, or is someone traveling with you?" The man peered up over his glasses as he handed her a pen and inkwell.

Constance dipped the nib into the black liquid, then proceeded to write her name on the register. "I'm alone." She opened her reticule and glanced up. "How much is the room?"

After he told her, she pulled out enough money to pay for a week, careful not to let anyone see how much she had left. Traveling alone was frightening enough without giving someone a reason to rob her.

Her room was on the second floor of the hotel, facing the street. She unpacked her carpetbag and placed the items in the chest of drawers beside the door. The pitcher on the washstand contained fresh water, so she was able to take care of her toilette.

Even though it was not quite evening, the strain of the journey pulled Constance toward the inviting bed. She laid down and closed her eyes, expecting to fall asleep immediately. However, her thoughts returned to the incident in the street. When she had missed the step, fear shot through her like an arrow, lancing the carefully constructed wall around her heart.

As the memory assailed her, Constance

once again felt that strong arms were lifting her. She had never been so close to any man except her father . . . and he hadn't carried her in his arms since she was a small child. She didn't understand the flurry of emotions that scattered through her. Nothing settled them until her gaze connected with the man's beautiful blue eyes.

Could she call a man's eyes beautiful? Well, no matter. His were. And his expression held a special kindness that Constance wasn't ready to analyze. She hoped she would never see him again. At the same time, she hoped she would. Confusion ruled her thoughts, and she fell asleep dreaming about a tall blond man.

Morning sunlight pulled Constance from a deep sleep. For a moment, she didn't know where she was. Not in the mountain cabin on a mattress tick filled with corn shucks. When she turned over, nothing rustled, and the softness of the featherbed caressed her body in comfort. After she opened her eyes and looked around the room, which seemed luxurious to her, a loud rumble from her stomach reminded her how long it had been since her last meager meal. While she hurried to dress, the fragrance of bacon and biscuits from somewhere below teased her senses.

When Constance reached the dining room on the first floor of the hotel, the room was almost empty. She wasn't used to sleeping this late. While she stood poised in the wide doorway between the hotel lobby and the restaurant, a grandmotherly woman swathed in a large apron came through the door from what had to be the kitchen.

"Well, come on in if you're hungry." The woman's smile lit her eyes with laughter. "You've come to the right place." She ushered Constance to an empty table by one of the front windows. "Would you like bacon, eggs, and biscuits or flapjacks?"

"What are flapjacks?" Constance couldn't help looking puzzled.

"Some people call them pancakes or griddle cakes. I like to make them with buckwheat, and we have real maple syrup, not just cane syrup."

"That sounds good." Once again, Constance's stomach made a loud protest.

"I'll be right back." The woman bustled through the door and returned immediately with a mug and a pot of coffee. "Would you like a cup?"

While she sipped the hot beverage, Constance studied the street outside the window. Browning City was larger and busier than the small town near the home place. People on horseback, in wagons and buggies, and walking on the boardwalks all seemed to have a purpose. Constance had a hard time imagining all she had seen in her journey. Even though she had read about these things in the books that filled the school library, to see them for herself made her feel almost giddy. To think, she probably never would have ventured as far as Fort Smith if her father hadn't extracted the promise from her. How was she ever going to find Jim Mitchell?

Constance didn't look forward to trying to get information about the man. People might get the wrong idea if she were too obvious with her questions. While she ate the wonderful flapjacks and bacon the waitress brought her, she devised a plan. She would make her way unobtrusively through the town, listening to conversations, trying to hear something about Jim Mitchell or his family. She didn't want anyone else to know about the gold before Mr. Mitchell had a chance to give it back on his own. That way, he might not get into trouble with the law.

Hans was striding toward the mercantile

when he noticed the woman from the stage crossing the street. Morning sunlight gleamed on the shiny curls that peeked out from under the brim of her bonnet. He'd heard his mother call that style coal shuttle. The way it tipped up in the back made the young woman look almost saucy.

He quickly glanced toward the front windows of the store so she wouldn't see him staring at her. *Wonder what she's doing in Browning City?* Would she stay long?

The bell over the door announced his entrance into the store where a customer could find almost anything. Hans moved toward the area where the proprietor kept nails. He had bent several this morning. For some reason, his aim must be off. Of course, he hadn't gotten as much rest last night as usual. The remembered feeling of that woman's soft body in his arms burned in his mind, chasing away sleep. Her lovely face with the large, multicolored eyes had beguiled him. He tossed and turned for hours before finally drifting into an uneasy slumber filled with dreams about an elusive woman who beckoned to him, then flitted away.

Hans shook his head and read the sizes written in pencil on the sides of the tins holding nails. Maybe he should get several different kinds. The bell above the door rang again, pulling his attention from the small metal spikes.

She had come into the mercantile, too.

Even though he turned back toward the hardware, the fragrance of flowers that accompanied her wafted toward him, reminding him of his torment during the night. Hans tried to keep his attention on what he was doing, but he was aware of her every move even though he didn't turn to follow her with his gaze. She glided around the store, stopping to finger different merchandise.

Several other customers clustered around the space, carrying on conversations. The woman moved near a group and looked at things on shelves nearby. When Hans glanced at her, she seemed to be paying more attention to the people than the merchandise. She looked up and noticed him studying her, so she moved on. She stopped near another group of people, fingering fabric as she covertly watched them.

Something didn't feel right to Hans. Was the woman trying to steal something? Surely she couldn't be a thief. He wanted to make sure, so he angled his body to where he could observe her without her knowing it.

Of course, that put him near things he wouldn't be interested in, not in a million years. He just didn't want the proprietor to be taken advantage of by this woman . . . and he didn't want to believe that she could be dishonest — a pretty woman like her with a delicate air about her and the hint of some hurt lurking behind her eyes.

When she moved on, nothing was missing from the shelf, and her handbag was so tiny, it wouldn't hold much if she did try to stuff anything in it. But something about her didn't seem quite right. Her movements looked furtive, as if she had something to hide.

Finding Mr. Mitchell might be more difficult than Constance had thought. Although she spent almost an hour in the general store, listening to see if anyone would mention the Mitchell family, not one person did. Perhaps she should go elsewhere.

Out on the sidewalk, Constance decided to explore the town a little more. She walked the other way down the street, stopping to peer into windows when it was possible to do so without drawing attention to herself.

Soon she had passed several businesses

and found her way into an area where houses lined the streets. One of them had a sign out front that proclaimed Barker's Boardinghouse. If Constance didn't find the Mitchells fairly soon, she might move there instead of staying at the hotel. Although her father had quite a bit of money saved, the cash wouldn't last forever.

She returned to the business section of town, hoping to eavesdrop on other conversations. A number of people milled around. She meandered about, trying to listen to conversations, but nothing helped her in her quest.

On one street, Constance noticed a school set a couple of blocks from a church. Back home in Arkansas when the circuit-riding preacher came through, they held services in the schoolhouse. She had never been in a building that was just a church. Maybe she would visit on Sunday, which was five days away.

Constance spent the next four days casually exploring the town, listening in on conversations but keeping her distance from people. One day, she went down a street that led to the livery stable. Just past that, a blacksmith shop stood with its wide doors flung open to the spring breezes. She stopped and quietly observed the man who had caught her when she fell. He pounded on red hot metal, forming what looked like a horseshoe. No wonder he had no trouble helping her. The strength she had felt in his arms made his work look easy, even though she knew it probably wasn't. Why was she spending so much time thinking about and observing him? No other man had ever spent so much time in her thoughts.

When Hans glanced up and saw the woman standing under the spreading branches of a tree down the street, he stopped hammering against the anvil. If he didn't, he would probably miss and smash his hand. It had taken all his willpower this week to keep his thoughts from dwelling on the way he had felt when he carried her the short distance from the stage to the boardwalk. While he stood staring, she turned and started back toward the center of town.

Hans plunged the horseshoe in cold water. Steam hissed up around him, bringing sweat to his brow. After placing the finished item on his worktable, he wiped his forearms and face with a towel and rolled down his sleeves. He pulled the doors closed and hurried up the street to follow the woman. Today, he intended to talk to her. Enough of this cat-and-mouse game they had been playing.

He almost caught up with her when she stopped to look at something in a store window. She turned and started back toward him, so Hans leaned against the front of the café in the next block. He heard a commotion in the alley that separated the two buildings and stuck his head around the corner of the building just as two boys started running toward the street. They weren't looking where they were going, and they should reach the end of the boardwalk about the time the woman would step down from it. If they collided with her, they would knock her into the dirt.

"Now where do you scallywags think you're going?" He grabbed each boy by the collar.

They turned angry eyes toward him.

"What are you doing, Mister?" The tallest boy sounded belligerent.

Hans looked up in time to see the woman smile at the three of them. "I'm just trying to keep you from running into this lady."

The boys stopped resisting and glanced up at her. "I'm sorry," they said in unison.

She turned her smile on them. "It's all right. You didn't see me coming, did you?"

They shook their heads and thanked her

before moving more sedately down the street, at least for a little ways.

"Thank you for saving me again." Her rich melodious words stretched between them, making an indefinable connection.

Hans felt tongue-tied, something he had never before experienced. He nodded.

She held out her hand. "My name is Constance Miller."

He looked at it a moment before engulfing it in his. "And I'm Hans Van de Kieft. I'm . . ."

"The blacksmith." She finished his sentence when he faltered. "I saw you working in your shop earlier." She looked down at their still-joined hands and gently extracted hers. "I'm glad to finally know your name."

While Hans watched Constance walk away, his heart thundered in his chest, and his stomach tied in knots again. He needed to talk to someone, so he started toward the parsonage. Hopefully, Jackson was home and had time to visit.

The pastor opened the door after the first knock. "Hans, come in. Mary has gone to the store or I would offer you something to eat."

Hans shook his head. "I'm not hungry." He was afraid that if he tried to eat, he wouldn't be able to swallow a bite. Of course, the sensation in his midsection wasn't exactly unpleasant.

"Well, that's a first, isn't it?" His best friend led the way into the parlor. "Is this just a social call in the middle of a workday, or did you come for a specific reason?"

Hans dropped into his favorite chair and leaned his forearms against his thighs, letting his hands dangle between his knees. "I kind of wanted to talk to you."

Jackson sat down and leaned back in his chair, resting one ankle on the other knee. "As a pastor or as a friend?"

"Both, I think."

"This sounds intriguing." Jackson's eyebrows rose in question. "How can I help you?"

It took a moment for Hans to verbalize his feelings. "Did you hear about me keeping that lady from falling from the stagecoach?" After his friend nodded, he continued, "Odd things have been happening to me since then. I'm not sleeping well, and when I do, I have strange dreams." He wasn't sure he had expressed himself in a way that could be understood.

Jackson didn't comment, just waited for him to continue.

"Actually, I just met her again, and when she shook hands with me, I had the same reactions I had when I caught her." He looked up hopefully, then back down at the floor.

"What kind of reactions?"

"I don't know. She's on my mind a lot, and I feel unsettled."

Jackson gave a soft snort, so Hans looked at him again. Jackson was trying not to laugh.

"Are you crazy or something?" Hans surged to his feet and moved around the room. "It's not funny. You're my pastor as well as my friend. I need to know what to do about these . . . feelings. I've always been able to control my emotions. Actually, no other woman has caused so much havoc in them. I know what lust is, and I don't believe that's what I feel, but I wonder if it's more than I should be feeling. I really want to get to know her, but I'm not sure she's honest."

A sober expression replaced the smile on Jackson's face. "I didn't mean to make light of what's happening to you. It's not a sin to want to get to know a woman. She may be passing through town, or she may be looking for a home here." He stopped for a moment as if mulling over something. "Just what about her makes you think she's not honest?"

Hans rubbed a hand across the back of his neck. "Nothing specific. I've seen her at the store a couple of times, and she didn't buy anything. She seemed to be listening in on conversations."

"Are you sure?"

Hans pictured the times, running through every move she made. "No, I'm not. But is it wrong to feel drawn to her since I don't know anything about her?"

THREE

Bright spring sunshine gave Sunday a heavenly glow, increasing the intensity of the color of new leaves on the trees and of multicolored buds peeking between greenery on the ground. Constance felt confident that she would look as good as anyone else at the church service because she was wearing another of the dresses she had purchased before she left Fort Smith. Her straw bonnet was decorated with silk flowers that complemented the light green ribbon matching her gown. She had never worn a pair of white cotton gloves before, but the woman at the store assured her that most women wore them to church. Of course, Constance wondered how they kept them clean. Maybe she would remove them and put them in her reticule when she was in the building.

She loved all the beauty of the day, but something about this prairie land made her feel unsettled. The mountains back home seemed to hold the sky high above her. Here there was so much blue spread from horizon to horizon that it almost pressed down against her. She wished for a few peaks to lift it up.

As she approached the building with its steeple topped by a small cross that stretched toward the heavens, she was glad to see so many other people streaming toward it. Many walked in family groups, but others rode horses or wagons. A few had fancy buggies such as she had never seen before.

Although Constance wouldn't be in Iowa long, she might like to meet a few other Christians. Back home, the circuit-riding preacher didn't get to their settlement more than once a month. On the other Sundays, her family and their neighbors had an all day singing and dinner on the grounds. It was the highlight of the week, a time when everyone rested from the hard labor of their days and enjoyed Christian fellowship. Constance missed a lot of those gatherings while her father was sick, and she left home soon after he was buried. She shed her tears of grief during the long hours of the night, because her days were busy.

She had traveled first to Fort Smith, where

she had spent a couple of weeks obtaining her wardrobe and learning about travel by stagecoach and about the state of Iowa. After that, she had headed to Browning City. During that time, Constance had felt very alone, afraid of the people around her. Not one of them had reached out to her. Hopefully, today would be different. She knew she could trust people who loved God.

When she entered the building, light from outside came through the frosted window-panes that lined the sides of the room. A single, stained-glass window above the hand-carved pulpit drew her attention. The Good Shepherd held a tiny sheep in His arms against His snowy robe. As a child, she had heard the story behind the picture. Constance walked down the center aisle and chose a seat about halfway toward the front of the sanctuary. She slipped off her cape, folded it, and placed it on the bench beside her. Then she removed her gloves and put them in her reticule on top of the cape.

Constance continued to study the picture, finally noticing other tiny sheep dotting the hillside in the background behind Jesus. Flowers scattered around His feet. She had never seen anything as beautiful as the window, and she basked in the warmth it brought to her heart. A faint hope rose that

God would take care of her and help her keep the promise to her father.

Soon after she sat down, the service began. When the pastor finished the opening prayer, a woman went to the pump organ, and a profusion of musical notes filled the room. The hymns they sang were familiar to Constance, so she joined in with all her heart.

When she put her wrap on the seat beside her, it made an effective barrier between her and those who shared the same pew. Not having someone sitting with her didn't detract from her enjoyment of the service. By the time the pastor started his message, she was glad she had come, even though she didn't know anyone.

" 'The secret things belong unto the LORD our God. . . .' " The pastor read a verse from Deuteronomy that Constance had never noticed before. " 'But those things which are revealed belong unto us and to our children for ever, that we may do all the words of this law.' "

Of course, Constance loved the New Testament, and she read it much more often than she did the Old Testament. But these words spoke straight to her heart. Too bad Mother's Bible had fallen apart more than a year before. If she still had it, she would look up the words and read them for herself. While the preacher continued his message, Constance started to pray silently that God would help her find Mr. Mitchell. She could conclude her business with him and return to her beloved mountains before very long.

Since Hans had started having a hard time going to sleep, sometimes he overslept. Because of this, he slipped into the church after the singing started and took a seat on the back pew. He didn't usually sit that far back. It made him feel as if he were a spectator instead of a participant in the service. He liked to be close to the front so nothing would distract him from worship. Jackson was a biblical scholar, and his messages always gave Hans a lot to think about. Often, he would return home and reread the passage of Scripture and mull over Jackson's words for days, noting how they applied to his own life.

When he was settled in his seat, Hans glanced toward the front. His attention snagged on a woman sitting about halfway down on the opposite side of the aisle. The tilt of her head and set of her shoulders caused his heartbeat to accelerate. He glanced down and took a deep breath before raising his head again. There were other single women in the congregation, but none made him feel this way.

Besides, maybe Constance Miller wasn't single. Just because no one came with her didn't mean that she didn't have a husband back home. At that thought, something unsettling dropped into his chest.

She probably was a believer. She sang every word of the hymns without looking at a hymnbook. The church only had a few scattered around the pews anyway.

Hans noticed that no one sat beside her. For just an instant, the idea of taking that empty space entered his mind, but he dismissed it, turning his attention to the words of the song. How could he be so interested in a woman he might not be able to trust? Besides, it would start gossip about both of them.

After the final prayer, Constance picked up her cape and fastened it around her shoulders before gathering her handbag and gloves.

"Hello." The cheery feminine voice came from behind her.

Constance turned to see a woman not much older than herself. A smile wreathed the petite woman's face.

"I'm Mary Reeves." She held out her

hand. "I don't believe I've met you."

While she took the proffered hand, Constance replied, "I just came to town last Monday. My name is Constance Miller."

The other woman gestured toward the back door where the pastor was shaking hands with people as they left the building. "That's my husband, Jackson. We'd like to have you join us for lunch. I have a roast in the oven, and we usually invite anyone who is new to share a meal with us."

Constance liked the woman's sincere smile. Maybe having dinner with them would be a good thing. She might find out something about the Mitchell family that way.

"Thank you."

As they made their way toward the door, Mrs. Reeves introduced Constance to several other women. They each welcomed her to both the church and the town. Maybe Constance would be able to make a few friends while she continued her quest.

It wasn't unusual for Jackson and Mary to invite Hans to eat with them, so he gladly accepted Jackson's invitation. As a single man, he always welcomed a home-cooked meal.

"I'll be there in a few minutes." Hans

squinted against the bright sunlight. "I finished fixing that kettle for Mary. I'll go fetch it. I know how much she uses it."

While he strode toward his shop, his thoughts returned to the Miller woman. There was some mystery about her, some secret she kept hidden. Why did she invade his thoughts so much? He didn't need to get involved with anyone who wasn't completely honest, did he?

He stepped up on the porch to the parsonage, and Jackson opened the door before he could put the kettle down and knock. "I watched for you. I know that thing is pretty heavy."

When Hans walked through the doorway, he almost dropped what he was carrying. The woman who had filled his thoughts and dreams so much this week sat in a kitchen chair talking with Mary.

"Come on in, Hans," Mary called from the kitchen. "I've invited Miss Miller to share our meal."

Miss? Mary called her *Miss.* Hans could only hope she was right. That is, if he really were interested in the woman.

When Mary started to introduce Constance to the blacksmith, Constance stopped her. "We've met. Mr. Van de Kieft has protected me from harm more than once."

She should have known that the other woman wouldn't let the subject drop. After they were seated, Mary wanted to know all about it. While they enjoyed the wonderful food, Constance and Hans had to recount both instances. It was interesting to hear the experiences from his perspective. By the time they were through with the stories, all four of them were laughing, and the atmosphere felt much more relaxed.

Constance offered to help Mary wash the dishes, but the other woman insisted that they leave them soaking in the dishpan. "I can wash dishes anytime. I want the chance for us to sit down and really get to know one another."

Mary brought cups of strong coffee into the parlor on a tray that also contained ginger cookies.

"Thanks, Mary." Hans took a couple of the large sweets in one hand. "These are my favorites."

"That's why I made them yesterday."

Constance wondered why the large man had such a strange expression on his face, as if he was surprised by what the pastor's wife said.

"But Jackson just invited me after the service." Hans sank his teeth into the cookie and sighed around it.

"Oh, I know, but we talked about it yesterday." Mary smiled at her husband, and Constance felt a sudden longing for someone to love like that. "But we didn't know that Miss Miller would be attending church this morning. Wasn't that a pleasant surprise?"

For some reason, Constance got the feeling that they weren't surprised at all. Now why did she feel that way?

Mary sat demurely on the sofa beside her husband. "So where exactly did you come from?"

Constance was just taking a sip of the hot beverage, and the abruptness of the question almost made her choke. Mary certainly got right to the point. "I've lived in the Ozark Mountains of northern Arkansas all my life."

Hans set his cup down on the coffee table and leaned back in his chair. "So what made you leave Arkansas?" His eyes narrowed, and she got the feeling that her answer was very important to him.

She glanced around the room, then out the front window. "This is a pretty area."

Constance turned back and took a nibble of her cookie. Looking at him out of the corner of her eye, she could tell that her answer didn't satisfy him. Constance was beginning to like this man, but she wasn't sure she wanted him asking too many personal questions.

Mary reached over and patted Constance's hand. "Wasn't it rather dangerous to travel alone? Didn't you have anyone to come with you?"

Tears sprang into Constance's eyes, and she tried to blink them back. "My mother has been gone for several years, and I . . . lost my father recently."

"Oh, I'm sorry." Mary's expression contained distress. "I didn't mean to bring up sad memories."

Constance swallowed a couple of times, trying to dislodge the lump in her throat. "It's part of life that you have to get used to."

Finally, Jackson joined the conversation. "That doesn't make it any less sad for the person who experiences the loss. Can I pray for you?"

When Constance nodded, they all bowed their heads. Jackson's prayer contained words of comfort that helped her move beyond the pain of the moment. When he finished, they sat for a few silent minutes. She had about decided that it was time for her to leave, but Hans cleared his throat.

"So why did you come to Browning City?"

What could she say without giving too much information? Constance groped in her mind for some way to answer truthfully. She stood and walked over to peer out between the curtains. Trying to find out something about the Mitchells by listening unobtrusively hadn't worked. Maybe she could trust her secret to these people . . . or at least part of it.

"Hans." Mary's voice sounded gentle. "Maybe Constance doesn't want to tell us. We shouldn't put her on the spot like that."

Constance turned toward the group. "That's okay. My father asked me to come find his friend from the war." She clasped her hands tightly in front of her waist. "Do any of you know Jim Mitchell?"

Jackson looked from his wife to Hans then back. "I believe a family by that name owned some land near the Mississippi River, but I don't think anyone has lived on the farm for more than a year."

Constance returned to her chair and perched on the front of it, clasping her hands in her lap. "Is it very far from here?"

"We're several miles from the Mississippi, and if I remember right, the farm is northeast from here." Jackson shuffled his feet against the rug. "I'm sorry we couldn't be any more help than that."

She stood and looked toward the hall tree where her cape hung. "You've helped me a lot. I needed friends, and you welcomed me into your home and fed me a delicious meal. But it's time I got back to the hotel."

Mary followed her into the foyer. "I hope we can become good friends."

"Thank you. I would like that."

Constance donned her cape and gloves and slipped out the door. She knew she was running away, but she had always been totally honest. Trying to keep a secret was becoming a burden to her heart.

Hans didn't stay long after Miss Miller left. He couldn't even remember what Jackson, Mary, and he had discussed in those last moments. His mind was on the story that Constance had told them and on the part of the story she left out. *Why is she so intent on finding this man? Is she interested in him in a romantic way?*

That thought felt like a spike sinking through his chest. He didn't care what she did. But she should be too young for her father's friend, shouldn't she?

FOUR

After leaving the parsonage, all Constance could think about was the fact that a Mitchell family owned a farm close to the Mississippi River, not too far from Browning City. That was probably Jim Mitchell's family. How could she find out? The question was her first thought on awakening Monday morning.

She paced from one side of her hotel room to the other trying to think what her father would do if he wanted to find them. Surely, he would go out there to the farm to see if anyone had returned. He might even try to get into the house and see if they left any indication where they might be. Constance could do that, couldn't she? Or maybe talk to a neighbor who might know where they went and when they would come back.

How would she find the farm? She didn't know anything about Iowa, except the portion she had seen from the windows of the stagecoach. If she had it figured out right, the Mississippi was east of Browning City. Did one of the roads lead east out of town? She could just follow that. Maybe it would be a good idea to talk to the sheriff and see if he knew where the farm was. She didn't want to ask Pastor Jackson and Mary about it again. It wouldn't do to arouse too much attention from anyone. They might ask more questions than she wanted to answer.

Constance went to the open window and leaned out to check the temperature. The spring breeze didn't feel cold, so she didn't put on her cape, just her bonnet, before picking up her reticule and going downstairs.

Thankfully, the hotel wasn't on a street where she could see the smithy. While she made her plans, the blacksmith's face often intruded on her thoughts. He didn't really know much about her. Although he had been kind to her, she knew he couldn't possibly be interested in her except as a casual friend. It wouldn't do any good to pay much attention to him. After she found Jim Mitchell, she would be on her way back to her beloved Ozarks.

The walk to the sheriff's office didn't help clear her jumbled thoughts. The door to the office stood open, so she stepped inside. The sheriff had his back to the door, tacking up a wanted poster. Constance had never been in such an office before. The room had a utilitarian feel to it, bare of decorations, unless you wanted to count the posters. They made her shiver in disgust. She didn't want to see outlaws, even if they were mostly drawings. She cleared her throat.

The sheriff whirled around. "Well, what can I do for you, little lady?"

Constance didn't like being called *little lady*. "My name is Constance Miller, and I've come for some information."

The sheriff held out his hand. "I'm Andrew Morton, and I'll help you if I can."

She barely touched his hand with her fingers when they shook hands. "I'm trying to find someone."

The sheriff took off his hat and laid it on his desk. "Have a seat." He gestured toward the chair in front of the desk while he leaned against the front corner of the large, plain wooden piece of furniture. "Who are you looking for?"

Constance cleared her throat again, this time because it felt so dry. "One of my father's army buddies. Jim Mitchell."

He scratched his stubbled cheek and stared into space for a moment. "I think he's the son of a family that owns a farm near the Mississippi."

"That's what I heard."

"I haven't seen hide nor hair of any of the Mitchells for almost a year." He moved behind the desk and dropped into his squeaky chair. "Why do you want to find Jim?" He leaned his arms on the desk and stared intently at her.

Constance squirmed, trying to find a more comfortable position on the hard wooden seat that was so tall her toes barely touched the floor. "My father wanted me to find him. Before he died, he made me promise to do that."

"I'm real sorry to hear about your father. When did you lose him?"

Tears sprang to Constance's eyes, and she removed a hanky from her reticule and blotted them away. "Several weeks ago."

The expression on the sheriff's face turned sympathetic. That brought more tears to Constance. She was sure that by now her nose and eyes must be red-rimmed. She blotted them again with the now soggy bit of cloth.

"Would you like me to go look for him?" He began tapping a pencil on the wooden desk in a brisk cadence. "I probably could go next week."

Constance stood. "No, thank you. If you

could just tell me how to get to the farm, I'll go myself."

He rolled up out of his chair and towered over her. "I can give you directions, but I'm not sure it's a good idea for you to go out there alone. I know you came on the coach by yourself —"

"How do you know that?" She knew it wasn't polite to interrupt, but she wanted to know where she stood with this lawman.

He chuckled. "I was standing with Hans when the coach drove up."

"I suppose you saw me fall." Constance knew how to make her tone icy. Hopefully, the man would take the hint.

His grin widened. "Actually, you didn't exactly fall. After you stumbled, Hans —"

As if their words called him, the blacksmith stepped through the doorway. "Andrew, I finished shoeing your horse, so I decided to bring him —" He stopped short and glanced from the sheriff to Constance.

The room felt extremely warm. She wished she had brought her fan. Hopefully, she didn't look too flushed. She even thought about grabbing one of those wanted posters and fanning herself with it.

"Hans." The sheriff skillfully took control of the conversation. "Miss Miller came to ask directions to the Mitchell farm. She wants to go there by herself. I was just starting to tell her it really isn't safe for a single young woman to travel out in the country alone."

Hans nodded. "I agree. Outlaws occasionally roam the back roads. She would be easy prey for them."

Constance stood as tall as she could, stiffening her back. "Thank you for your concern, but I don't want to wait until next week when the sheriff could check it out for me. I want to finish my business with Mr. Mitchell and return home as soon as possible." She turned toward the lawman. "If you'll be so kind as to give me the directions . . . maybe you could write them down, so I won't get lost."

The sheriff sat back down and pulled a tablet and pencil from the top drawer of his desk. "I can't stop you from going, so I'll write the directions so you won't get lost, but I still don't think it's a good idea.

"I'll go with her."

Hans stuck his hands in the back pockets of his trousers. So much for forgetting about Constance Miller. Not only would she be in his thoughts, he was going to spend at least a day with her.

"Oh, but I couldn't take you away from

your work." She started to reach for his arm, but then let her hand drop. He followed her actions with his gaze.

He turned to look in her beautiful face, a face that held a very becoming blush. "Work's a mite slow right now." He watched her indecision dissolve into acceptance. "It might take most of the day, so I'll pick you up at the hotel at nine o'clock in the morning, if that's all right with you."

Her nod was almost imperceptible.

"Here are the directions." Andrew handed the piece of paper to him. "I think you know where this is."

Hans studied the notes and crude drawing. "Ja, I know the place. We won't have any trouble finding it." He stuck the paper in his shirt pocket and turned to go.

"Thank you, Mr. Van de Kieft." Her soft words followed him into the street, the melody of them once again playing on his heart.

As expected, Hans didn't get much sleep that night, either. At one point, he stood by his bedroom window and stared at the stars. "Vader God, why is this happening to me?"

When he spoke out loud to the Lord, he wished for an audible answer in return, but it didn't come. However, peace stole over his heart. Maybe God had everything under control. Maybe it was His will for Hans to spend time with this woman.

Since she had expressed her desire to return to Arkansas, he needed to guard his heart. If he got too close to her, he would be hurt when she left. When he finally fell asleep, he slept longer than he planned and had to hurry to get everything ready to pick her up.

Nine o'clock had passed when he pulled the wagon up in front of the hotel. While he tied the reins to the hitching post, Constance came out on the boardwalk.

"Will I need a parasol to protect me from the sun?"

Because the walkway was a couple of feet from the level of the street, Hans had to look up at her. "Yes, bring one. The road we'll follow has shade in some places, but not in others."

He stood with his hands fisted on his hips and watched her go back into the building. Her clothes were more sensible for a ride than anything he'd seen on her so far. The brown skirt and matching top wouldn't show the dust too much, and the fullness of the skirt would make it easier for her to get up into the wagon. Of course, he would be glad to help her. As tiny as she was, he could just swing her up. That thought reminded him of the other times he had touched her. The familiar knot tied itself in his midsection.

As soon as they passed the edge of town, trees lined the roadway. Even though the leaves on many were just coming out, they provided respite from the sun. Constance folded her sunshade and laid it behind her in the conveyance. "What's this stuff in the back of the wagon?"

She eyed the folded quilt as if it were a coiled serpent. After she returned to the hotel yesterday, all kinds of doubts tormented her. Could she really trust this man? He had protected her from harm twice before, but were his intentions honorable today? Maybe possible outlaws weren't the only danger on the trip.

"It will take us more than an hour to reach the farm." The man didn't take his eyes off the road when he talked to her. "The basket contains food for our lunch, and I brought the quilt in case we have to eat on the ground."

"Thank you." She was always thanking the man. Why hadn't she realized that they would need to eat while they were gone? She could have asked the hotel kitchen to prepare them something. If she were back home, she would have known what to do. Here she felt almost like a fish out of water. Everything was topsy-turvy, and she didn't always think straight.

They rode along for more than an hour without saying anything. Constance watched the countryside change from fairly flat land with lots of trees to small rolling hills with tall grasses blowing in the wind. Soon after they left the shelter of sparse shade, she once again unfurled her parasol. Holding it kept her hands busy.

Mr. Van de Kieft wasn't talkative. At first, she was glad. What did they have to talk about anyway? Then she decided that he was either just being stubborn or he was ignoring her. She didn't like to feel ignored.

"Have you always lived in Browning City?" Her question must have startled him, because he gave a slight jump.

He turned toward her and studied her expression for a moment. "Not always."

Was that all he was going to say? "So where did you live before?"

He kept his eyes on the road ahead. "My family came here from the Netherlands when I was only ten years old. We had a farm north of Browning City."

Once again, silence stretched between them. When it became uncomfortable to

Constance, she asked another question. "You said 'had.' Are they not there now?"

When he shook his head, the shiny blond hairs that barely touched his collar stirred in the soft breeze. "No. My father's only brother and his family came to America after we did. He settled in Pennsylvania. My parents decided to move close to them."

Constance stared at him. "And you didn't go with them?"

He guided the horses around a bend in the road before he answered. "I was serving as an apprentice to the blacksmith and didn't want to go." He glanced at her as if looking for her reaction.

"Do you hear from them?"

"Ja, we write letters all the time."

When they finally turned down the lane that led to the farm, Constance was glad Hans had thought to bring food. Her stomach gave a very unladylike rumble.

"Are you hungry?" His words surprised her, because he hadn't said anything for quite a while.

"I believe I am." *How embarrassing!* Because they were once again riding in speckled shade, she folded her parasol and put it behind her.

"We should be at the house pretty soon.

Let's check to see if anyone is living there first."

They soon rounded a bend in the lane that revealed a meadow reaching all the way to the edge of a bluff. Although she could hear the river flowing below, they seemed to be high above it. On the other side of the meadow, a house nestled between trees at the edge of a forest. What a beautiful setting for a home.

"The house looks deserted." Hans pulled on the reins, and the team came to a full stop. "If you want to, we could eat closer to the edge of the bluff, and you can take in the view."

She turned toward him. "That's thoughtful. I would enjoy it very much."

"The horses have plenty of grass to eat here. After we've finished our meal, I'll try to find some place to water them."

Hans set the brake and stepped over the side of the wagon. When he was on the ground, he turned and placed his hands on her waist. Before she realized what was happening, she stood on the ground beside him. It took a moment for her to catch her breath. The man really was strong to lift her so effortlessly over the side of the vehicle. The warm imprint of his hands on her waist lingered, making her uncomfortable.

He headed toward the back of the wagon, and she followed. "I can carry the quilt." She tried not to sound breathless but didn't quite make it.

"Mary was kind enough to fix the food for us." Hans smiled at Constance. "She said to tell you to enjoy it."

"I'll be sure to thank her the next time I see her."

Soon the quilt was spread under the shade of a tree far enough away from the edge of the bluff to be comfortably safe. Constance enjoyed the view while Hans unpacked the picnic basket. The tantalizing fragrance of fried chicken called to her stomach, and it rumbled a response.

"I can't exactly remember my geography. Is that area across the river still Iowa?"

Hans looked up from his task. "No. That's Illinois. The river is the eastern boundary of Iowa." He pulled a large jug of fresh water and two tin cups from the basket. "Our food is ready."

Constance sat on the other side of the quilt. Hans was glad he could face her and study her while they ate. After she finished arranging her skirt around her, he handed her a blue granite plate, a silver fork, and a red-checked napkin.

The food tasted wonderful out in the spring air. Besides the chicken, Mary had included biscuits, cheese, and pound cake. As they ate, their conversation took many turns, but they learned a lot about each other. For the first time, Hans felt really comfortable around Constance. Comfortable enough to ask the question that burned a hole in his heart and mind.

"Why did your father insist on you finding this Mr. Mitchell?"

Constance paused with her tin cup halfway to her mouth. Her gaze bore into his before she turned her eyes away from him. For a moment, he didn't think she was going to answer.

"He wanted me to give him a message."

"It must be a very important message." He waited for her response that never came.

The way she stayed turned away and wouldn't look at him confirmed the suspicions Hans harbored. There was much more to the story than she was willing to reveal. What was she hiding? If it wasn't something bad, why was she so secretive?

FIVE

Constance walked toward the house. Hans met her going the opposite direction, leading the horses to the spring-fed pool they found quite a ways into the woods. While he watered them, she gazed all around the meadow. The house looked pretty large. Maybe the Mitchell family needed a lot of space. She wondered how many people lived here.

Each side of the building contained at least two windows. She had never seen this many on a house in the country before. Hoping to get a look inside, she pushed aside the bushes that grew in every direction from their position beside the house. Unfortunately, curtains obstructed her view of the room. After trying two more windows and receiving several scratches on her hands, she gave up. She walked the perimeter of the house at a distance far enough away to avoid touching the prickly plants.

The walls looked sound. Constance stepped up on the front porch and turned around. Since the meadow gradually rose from the edge of the bluff to the level of the house, she could see far into the distance. Even though she missed the mountains, she would enjoy seeing a view like this every morning. Facing east, the morning sunlight would warm the house, but when the heat of the afternoon sun beat down, the trees surrounding three sides of the house would keep it cool.

Constance moved over by one of the narrow, square columns supporting the roof of the porch. If she owned a house like this, she would put a couple of rocking chairs out here. It would be a good place to sit in the evening, watching twilight creep across the landscape.

After enjoying this scenario, she turned to check the front door. If it wasn't locked, maybe she could slip into the house. She had never gone into anyone's house without them inviting her in, but the place was deserted. It wouldn't hurt to look around.

Just as the latch clicked open, Hans came around the side of the house. "It's time we started back."

Disappointed, she pulled the door closed again. She wanted to be alone when she checked out the house. At least now that she knew the way to the farm, she could come by herself.

After they were seated in the wagon, Hans clicked his tongue to the two horses. "There's another farmhouse not too far from here. Maybe we could stop and see if the neighbors know anything about this family."

Constance turned to look at him. "That would be helpful. Tha—" She gulped on that word.

"Constance, you don't have to thank me for every little thing I do." He sounded amused.

She gripped her hands in her lap. "My mother taught me to be polite." She peeked up at him.

He nodded, but she noticed he kept his thoughts to himself.

She did too. Constance had a lot to think about. Why would a family just leave such a nice place sitting empty? Where did they go? When did they plan to come back? Would they ever come back?

Hans turned the team onto a lane that led back through a copse of trees. He knew there was a farm on the other side. Soon the wagon emerged into an open field with a house on the east side.

"Hallo." His shout must have startled Constance, because she jerked and grabbed onto the seat. "Anybody home?"

A man carrying a pitchfork came out of the barn and started toward them with the tool across one shoulder. They met halfway to the house.

"What kin I do for you?"

Good, he was friendly. Hans knew that not all farmers liked people coming onto their land. Since this house was hidden from the road, he had been afraid the owner wouldn't welcome them.

Hans hopped out of the wagon and shook the man's hand. "We're trying to find out something about the Mitchell family who live between here and the river."

"You and your missus want to come up to the house for a cold drink of water?"

Hans knew that if the man knew they were unmarried and traveling alone, he would get the wrong idea about Constance, so he didn't correct the man. He wasn't sure Constance noticed. If she had any questions, he would answer them after they were on the road again.

"We had some just a bit ago. Thank you, anyway. What can you tell me about the Mitchells?"

"You're not the law, are you? No one's in trouble?"

Hans shook his head. "Constance's father wanted her to look up his army buddy, Jim."

The farmer stuck the pitchfork into the dirt and leaned one arm on the top. "Jim and his brother came back after the war." He pulled a bandanna out of the back pocket of his overalls and wiped the sweat from his forehead. "They was 'round here for a couple of years." He stuffed the handkerchief back into the pocket but left most of it hanging out, probably to dry.

"About a year ago, both the old man and his wife took real sick. The brothers tried to nurse them back to health, but it didn't work. After their parents died, those boys hightailed it out of here, and we ain't heard from them since." He put his other arm across the one on the handle of the tool. "Can I help you with anything else?"

Hans scuffed his toe through the dirt on the lane. "Has anyone else been interested in the farm?"

"Not so's I know. Jim and his brother asked us to look after the place for them. We keep an eye on it, but I haven't seen anyone nosing around."

Hans studied the man's expression. He felt sure the farmer was telling the truth, but since this farm was cut off from the road by all the trees, the man might not know if anyone went up there.

"Thank you for the information." Hans stuck out his hand, and the farmer shook it before hefting the pitchfork back across his shoulder.

The man pointed to a grassy area on the other side of the lane. "You can turn your wagon around over there. There ain't no soft spots where you kin get stuck."

Back out on the road, Constance finally spoke. "You didn't tell him we weren't married."

Hans nodded. "I know."

"Why not?"

He glanced at her to see if she looked angry. Thankfully, she didn't. "I thought it would be better for your reputation if he didn't think you were single."

"But isn't that lying?"

"I didn't tell a lie. I just let him think what he wanted to."

This conversation was taking them nowhere. Hans wished he could get her to open up to him and tell him the real reason she was so intent on finding Jim Mitchell. There could be all kinds of reasons. Maybe her father promised her to Mr. Mitchell, and he wanted her to fulfill the promise.

But she didn't look as if she were trying to find her intended.

Could there be some other, less legal reason she wanted to find the man? That thought kept nibbling at him, making him feel unsettled.

They arrived back in Browning City mid-afternoon. Constance felt tired. She didn't think she would have been so exhausted if she'd been able to get the man to carry on a conversation on the long trek. As it was, she felt that Hans didn't quite trust her. Maybe he guessed that there was more to her promise than she had told him. There was, but it wasn't really any of his business. Talking about unimportant things would have made the time go faster.

She tried to get him to notice the country they drove through. His monosyllabic answers effectively cut any conversation short. Constance would have just as well traveled alone for all the company he was.

Hans stopped the wagon in front of the hotel and hopped out. By the time Constance stood up, he was on her side of the wagon, ready to help her down. This time, he took her hand and held her steady as she stepped over the side onto a spoke of the front wheel.

When she stood on the ground, she looked up into his face. "I appreciate the way you helped me today."

"Constance . . . Hans." Mary came out the front door of the hotel. "I've been looking for you. I guess I didn't realize it would take this long to go to the farm." She stood on the boardwalk and smiled at them.

Hans offered Constance his arm and escorted her to the steps where the boardwalk broke for the alley. By the time they were at the top of the steps, Mary stood beside them.

Constance let go of his elbow and turned to the pastor's wife. "Why were you looking for us?"

"Actually, I was looking for you." Mary took Constance's arm and pulled her toward the hotel lobby. "Let's sit in here so I can tell you what I found out."

After the two women waved at Hans as he departed, they sat on a sofa beside one wall. A tall bushy plant made the spot feel secluded.

Mary looked as if she were about to explode with excitement. "Mrs. Barker owns the boardinghouse."

"I've noticed it on the other side of town."

"Well, she's a really good cook, but she doesn't like to bake. She had a woman who did all her baking, but the woman fell and broke her leg. Mrs. Barker needs another cook. I thought you might like to do it, if you know how to bake, that is. You would get a free room at the boardinghouse, and she'd pay you some, too." Mary talked so fast, Constance couldn't get a word in edgewise. "I know you won't be here long, but maybe you could stay until the other cook is on her feet and able to work again." When she stopped talking, she turned an expectant expression toward Constance.

Baking was one of Constance's favorite things to do, and she was good at it. She wanted to stay in town until she could locate Jim Mitchell, anyway. Maybe she should do something to bring in money instead of spending so much of her savings.

"That sounds like a good idea." Constance smiled at Mary, joining in her excitement. "I know how to bake lots of things."

Mary stood. "Do you want to go meet her right now?"

When they arrived at the boardinghouse, Mrs. Barker stood on the porch talking to a couple who rented a room from her. Mary and Constance waited on the front walkway until the trio finished their conversation.

"Mary Reeves," Mrs. Barker called from the porch. "What are you doing standing out there in the sun? Bring your friend up here for a cool drink of water."

Constance followed Mary up the steps, and the two women sat in inviting cushioned rocking chairs. These were just the kind Constance imagined should be on the front porch of the Mitchell's farmhouse.

"So what brings you here?" The proprietor of the boardinghouse dropped into the third rocker.

Mary leaned forward. "I want you to meet Constance Miller. She's new to town, and she knows how to bake."

At that last statement, Mrs. Barker's face beamed. "Does she now?" She peered at Constance over the top of her glasses. "Are you looking for a job?"

Constance wasn't sure why she felt so nervous. Maybe because she had never had a job in her life. "I understand you need someone for a while. I won't be here too long, but I could stay until your other cook comes back to work."

The older woman tented her fingers under her chin and stared out at the treetops across the street. After a moment, she turned back toward Constance. "So what exactly do you know how to bake?"

Constance had expected to be asked such a question, so she had a ready answer. "It's been said that my biscuits are the lightest ones in the holler back home. I always make berry pies in the summer. We dried peaches and apples so we had those kinds of pies all year round. No one has ever complained that my crusts were tough."

Mrs. Barker rocked her chair back and forth. "This is sounding better all the time. Is that all?"

"Well, my pa was partial to yeast rolls, but sometimes I made potato rolls or sourdough rolls when we couldn't get the yeast."

"My mouth is watering just from the telling." Mrs. Barker smacked her lips. "What about cakes?"

Constance didn't want to brag too much. She'd done enough of that in the last few minutes to last all year. But she needed to give Mrs. Barker enough information so she could make her decision.

"My pound cake always gets eaten first on Sundays when we have dinner-on-the-grounds. I can make other kinds, too. Apple spice, pumpkin, several others."

Mary rocked contentedly and gave Constance an encouraging smile.

"Would you be willing to show me what you can do?" Mrs. Barker sounded eager.

"Do you want me to make biscuits for dinner tonight? There's time." Constance felt a spark of excitement inside.

Mrs. Barker stood up. "Come right on in. Mary, are you going to stay and visit while we do this?"

The beef stew simmering in a large kettle on the back of the stove filled the kitchen with an enticing aroma. Constance realized with a start that she was hungry again. She would enjoy eating here.

"Since you're having stew" — Constance hooked one of Mrs. Barker's aprons over her head and tied it behind her back — "why don't I make a pan of cornbread, too?"

"Sounds good to me." Mrs. Barker started putting containers out on the table. Then she turned toward Mary. "You and Pastor Jackson would be welcome to stop by for supper."

After Mary agreed, she left, presumably to tell her husband about the invitation.

Mrs. Barker sat beside the table, greasing baking tins, while Constance got started mixing the dough. They chatted while they worked, and soon Constance knew she would like to live here and work for this woman.

When the first pan of lightly browned biscuits came out of the oven, Mrs. Barker exclaimed, "Constance, you have a job if you want one."

Constance dusted the last of the flour from her hands and smiled at the other woman. "I want one."

"Then you can move your things from the hotel after supper. Come upstairs, and I'll show you your room."

After dinner, Pastor Jackson and Mary walked back to the hotel with Constance. He waited in the lobby while the two women went upstairs. Constance pulled her carpetbag out from under the bed and carefully packed her belongings in it.

"I'm glad you could help Mrs. Barker this way." Mary stood by the window, gazing out into the twilit evening.

Constance stopped folding her unmentionables. "It'll help me, too. I won't have to be quite so careful with the rest of Pa's money." She went over to the other woman and gave her a quick hug. "Thank you."

Mary turned back toward her. "I can see God's hand in all of this, can't you?"

Constance nodded. Of course. How could she ever have gotten this far without God's help? But why couldn't she find Jim Mitchell, and why did God want her here in Browning City, Iowa, if she couldn't?

Six

Constance stood looking out the window of her upstairs room in the boardinghouse. A nearly full moon shone through the cold night air, lighting an inky sky that contained pin dots of stars. A soft breeze ruffled the leaves recently emerged from their buds on the trees. She felt so far from her mountain home.

Time and distance hadn't really dulled the pain of being alone. Even though she tried to keep all her grieving to the nighttime hours, some days it was extremely hard to keep up the strong front she maintained before others.

The little girl inside her wanted her mother back. Had it really been three years since Ma died? That event so soon after Pa returned from the fighting seemed to change him more than the war had. Maybe that was the reason he wasn't able to fight off his final illness.

Tears streamed down her cheeks, and she didn't bother to rub them away. Not only did she long for a comforting hug from her mother, she wished she were still a little girl who could climb up in her daddy's lap and lay her head on his shoulder. How safe she had felt there.

She turned back toward the pleasant room. Mrs. Barker made the rooms homey. Constance had never had things this nice when she grew up. Mother did make quilts out of the good parts of their worn-out clothes, and she used every scrap left over from making new things, but her quilts were more utilitarian than beautiful. Constance crossed the room and ran her fingers along the honeycomb pattern so different from Ma's nine-patch quilts.

If Pa had used more of the money he saved, they could have had nicer things. It wouldn't have been soon enough to save Ma, but . . . her mind couldn't even imagine what it would have meant.

The tears came faster, flowing down and spotting the multicolored cover. Constance pulled it back and slid between sheets smoother than she had ever slept on before. Even the ones in the hotel weren't this nice. She turned her face into the pillow to muffle her sobs and cried for her losses and for what might have been. But there was something more inside her that she couldn't explain. Some deep longing she had never felt before.

Because she slept fitfully, Constance was up before the chickens, as her mother would often say. She bathed her face in the cold water left in her pitcher, hoping it would erase the ravages of a night spent in grief. She peered into the looking glass above the washstand. Her skin only had a few red blotches on it. By the time she was dressed, more natural color filled her face.

Constance pasted on a smile, took a deep breath, and opened the door. When she reached the kitchen, it stood empty, silent, and lonely. She went to the black cast-iron stove and stirred the embers, adding more wood from the pile on the back porch. While the fire built up, she put ground coffee and water in the blue graniteware pot and set it on the back of the stove.

By the time Mrs. Barker came into the kitchen, the room had warmed, and the smell of fresh-brewed coffee filled the air. Constance stood beside the table, cutting biscuits from the dough she had patted out on its floured surface.

"Why, Constance." Mrs. Barker went over to pour herself a cup of coffee. "You don't have to get up so early. I usually stoke the fire and start the coffee." She turned and leaned against the cabinet that held the empty dishpan and a bucket of water.

Constance continued cutting the dough and putting the biscuits in a greased pan. "I woke early, so it didn't make any sense to lie abed." Although she didn't glance up, she could feel Mrs. Barker looking at her.

"I have a rolling pin."

Constance turned to look at her employer before concentrating on her task. "I don't really like to roll the biscuits. I know I did last night, but I was just getting used to this kitchen. They will be lighter if I don't work the dough too much. I just pat it to the thickness I want."

Mrs. Barker came over and glanced at those in the pan. "I never thought of doing something like that."

Once again, Constance felt the woman looking at her. She raised her head and smiled at her employer.

After setting her cup on the edge of the table away from where Constance worked, Mrs. Barker studied Constance's face as if she were reading a book. "I see a hint of sadness in your eyes that I didn't notice yesterday. Are you homesick for your family?"

Constance swallowed around the lump in her throat, a lump that was probably made up of more tears waiting to be released. "I don't have any family left." She sobbed on the last word.

"Oh, you poor dear."

The sympathy in Mrs. Barker's voice released some of that reservoir of tears. Constance reached up and swiped them away.

"I think you need a mother's hug."

Comforting arms engulfed Constance and didn't let go. She enjoyed them for a moment before she stepped back. "Thank you." Here she was thanking someone again. She stiffened her spine and went back to her task.

"I'm here for you anytime you need me." Mrs. Barker bustled over and placed a skillet on the stove. Then she started stirring eggs together to scramble.

At breakfast, Constance paid closer attention to catch the names of the people at the table. Two men named Theodore and Thomas sat beside each other. She could tell by all their similarities that they must be brothers. Short in stature, their balding heads had tufts of hair around the sides and back that stood straight up, and their eyes twinkled when they laughed. Not only did they look almost identical, their voices sounded similar, and their gestures followed the same patterns. They kept talking about working at the mercantile. From what they said, they must be employees, not the owners of the place.

Martha Sutter was the schoolteacher, and Sylvia Marshall talked about the clothing she designed for a customer, so she had to be a seamstress. Constance wondered where she did her work. The new couple who rented a room yesterday afternoon was quieter, listening to the others. However, when Martha asked their names, they told her they were Ed and Frances Owens. They didn't say much else except that they were looking for a farm to buy, so they might not live in the boardinghouse very long.

"Mrs. Barker, how is Selena?" Constance wondered who Sylvia was inquiring about.

"She's still in a lot of pain." The proprietress shook her head as if dismayed. "Her sister came in from their farm and took her home with her. She wanted to be sure she was well cared for. The doctor is concerned because the break wasn't a clean one. He's afraid it might take awhile to heal."

The other cook. Constance said a silent prayer for the woman.

Constance baked all morning. Mrs. Barker wanted bread so they could have sandwiches for supper. She gave Constance canned peaches to make pies for lunch, and Constance made a pound cake to have at suppertime. All the work felt good. It had been too long since she felt such a sense of accomplishment.

When everyone came in for supper, Hans arrived. He told Mrs. Barker that he wanted to eat at the boardinghouse that night. He was tired of his own cooking. Somehow, Constance had a hard time picturing the gentle giant toiling over a hot stove. She wondered what he cooked.

"You're welcome to eat here anytime." Mrs. Barker smiled encouragement at him. "I can always use the extra money."

Constance ate quietly, listening to all the conversations around the table. She hoped they would mention something that would help her finish her quest.

"Mrs. Barker, this pound cake is the best one I've ever eaten." Hans stuffed a forkful into his mouth, and a smile lit his face.

"Thank Constance." The woman gestured toward her. "She's my new baker."

Hans stared at Constance. "I didn't know you were looking for a job."

She dropped her hands into her lap. "I wasn't. Remember Mary was waiting to talk to me when we returned to town?" He nodded, and she continued. "That's what she wanted to tell me. That Mrs. Barker needed someone to bake while her cook recovered. It sounded good to me. I have a better place to stay than the hotel, and I can save my money."

"If you're going to bake every day, I just might have to eat here every night." Hans laughed.

Some of the others joined in. Their compliments about her baking abilities encouraged Constance. Maybe she was supposed to be here right now. If only someone would mention something about the Mitchell boys, especially Jim.

The thought of Hans eating here every night caused an unsettled feeling in her. Why did the prospect of seeing him every day make her happy?

Hans had been surprised to learn that Constance had a job at the boardinghouse. Pleasantly surprised, since the things she baked were so delicious. When he told Mrs. Barker he might eat there every night, he meant it as a joke. After she agreed, he knew it was just what he wanted to do. Maybe by being there with everyone sharing their days, he would be able to find out what Constance was hiding. And the food was far better than anything he put together.

For the next few nights, he showed up right when the meal was being served. Every night, Constance made a different kind of dessert. If Hans didn't work so hard, he might get fat eating all those rich sweets.

Since his family had moved away, he lived alone. He hadn't felt lonely until he spent so much time with other people around the table in the evening. Maybe he wasn't created to be solitary. He had friends, but when he went home after work, the evenings seemed to stretch on forever.

Today was Saturday, and several people from outlying farms who came to town to pick up supplies also brought items that he needed to repair for them. A couple even had him shoe more than one horse, which they would take home when they left town later. His day was long, almost past the supper hour at the boardinghouse.

When he arrived, everyone was finishing their meal and ready for dessert. He had just walked in as Mrs. Barker had told him to do, but when he saw all the empty dishes on the table, he turned to leave.

"Hans." Mrs. Barker hurried around the table to greet him. "I thought you would be coming. I told Constance to put a plate in the warming oven for you." She turned to look at the young woman. "Why don't you get it for Hans while I pour his drink?"

Constance carried the covered plate with two thick, quilted potholders. When she set it in front of him and lifted the cover, the smell of fried chicken, mashed potatoes, and gravy caused his stomach to rumble. He hoped no one noticed, but just before Constance turned away, he noticed a twinkle in her eye. It looked good there. Too often, her face held a sad expression.

Mrs. Barker patted Constance on the shoulder. "You sit down and finish your food. I'll get the apple pie for everyone."

Constance slipped into the empty chair beside him. He felt her presence so strongly that, even if his eyes had been closed, he would have known she was there.

Mrs. Barker returned carrying two plates of pie, which she set in front of the two single women who roomed with her. "What kept you so long, Hans?"

Everyone turned to look at him expectantly. He didn't like the feeling of being the center of attention. "I had lots of customers today. Then I went home to clean up. I didn't want to show up at your table in dirty clothes or with dirty hands."

A chorus of chuckles went round the table, and conversation resumed. Hans enjoyed the excellent food while everyone else except Constance ate dessert. One by one, they excused themselves and left the room. Then Mrs. Barker took her empty plates into the kitchen.

"I've been wanting to ask you something, Constance." When he said her name, she looked at him instead of the food on her plate. "I have a buggy, and I would like to pick you up and take you to church in the morning." Her expression told him that she might want to decline his invitation. "I know you walked last week, but the boardinghouse is farther away, and the weather is getting warmer. We could even ask Mrs. Barker if she wants a ride, too. Would that be all right with you?"

Constance stopped eating and put her fork down. After a long moment, she turned to smile at him. "That would be nice, Hans."

Mrs. Barker agreed to go to church with them, but she planned to go out to see Selena after the services. The people who lived on the neighboring farm to Selena's sister had offered to give her a ride out there and even bring her back to town.

On Sunday, the sanctuary of the church welcomed Constance like an old friend. How could she have gotten to feel so at home in such a short time? Hans stayed outside talking to one of the farmers, and that suited her fine. She sat in the same pew where she had sat the week before and looked up at the Good Shepherd. Mary turned around in the front row and smiled at Constance. Several times this week, the two women had spent time together.

Just before Pa came home from the war, Patience — Constance's best friend all through her growing-up years — had gotten married and moved to Little Rock. At first, they wrote letters to each other. Then when Patience and her husband had a baby, the letters became few and far between. It had been months since she had received one. Already, Mary had become a good friend to Constance, filling the hole left by losing Patience.

Before Jackson stood up for the opening prayer, Hans came down the aisle and asked her if he could sit beside her. She slid over and let him be by the aisle. Constance hoped no one got the wrong idea. Mary glanced back again, and her smile widened.

After the final prayer, Mary made a bee-line up the aisle, stopping beside Hans. "Jackson and I would like to invite the two of you over for lunch. Today, I left a meatloaf in the warming oven."

A big smile spread across the man's face. "I really like your meatloaf."

Constance wondered if there was any food he didn't like. She'd seen him eat a lot of every supper at the boardinghouse. She wondered if Mrs. Barker was charging him enough for his meals.

"So how about it, Constance?" Mary's eyes pleaded with her. "We really enjoyed last week."

Constance glanced around the room that was rapidly becoming empty. "Won't other people want to spend time with you, too? They might not like you spending so much time with someone new."

Mary's face held an incredulous expression. "No one will care. Most of these people hurry back to their farms to take care of livestock. Besides, we've had supper with three different families this week. So please say you'll come. I know Mrs. Barker doesn't serve meals to the boarders on Sunday."

How could she say no? Jackson had helped her start finding the Mitchell property, and

Mary had found her a job. Besides, she really enjoyed this couple. She glanced up at the tall man standing in the aisle beside her. If she were truthful with herself, she had to admit that spending time with Hans could be interesting, too. It couldn't hurt to do it one more time, could it?

Seven

"That man really does like your meatloaf." Constance laughed at the memory of Hans's appreciation.

At least today Mary let Constance help her with the dishes. While Mary washed, Constance dried and stacked them on the table. Later, she would help Mary put them up. Then next time she came, she would know where they went in the cupboard behind the curtains that hung above the dishpan.

Mary's eyes twinkled in amusement. "That's why I made such a large one. He did eat quite a bit, didn't he?" After plunging a plate in the rinse water, she shook off the excess and handed it to Constance. "He's been here before, but you have to agree that it takes a lot of food to fuel a man that large."

Constance felt the warmth of a blush make its way up her neck and into her cheeks. She had been thinking the same thing. Not only was Hans handsome, but he was also strong and well-built. Of course, a lady shouldn't have noticed a man's build, but how could she miss it? She placed the dry plate on top of the stack on the table and turned back around. His muscles rippled when he ate, as well as when he worked.

Mary had a speculative gleam in her lively eyes. She put her hands on her hips and laughed. "You already noticed that, didn't you?"

Constance tried to think of something to change the subject, but just then the topic of conversation came through the back door, accompanied by Jackson. "Here come the men." She ducked her head and polished an already shining piece of silverware.

Mary turned toward her husband. "So what did Hans think?"

Constance wondered what Mary meant. The men had stepped outside while the women cleaned up the table, but Constance hadn't known that there was an ulterior motive.

Jackson put his arm around his wife and pulled her close to his side. "He agrees with me. We can do it, and he will help."

"Help with what?" Constance laid the

damp towel on top of the cabinet beside the wash basin and folded her arms. "I'm missing something here."

Hans smiled at her, and for a moment, her breath caught in her throat. Then he turned toward Jackson. "Our pastor decided we should use the extra land behind the parsonage to start a large garden. Several members of the congregation don't have access to an area where they can grow vegetables. We could either let them help with the garden, or we could give some of the excess produce to those who need it most."

Jackson pulled at the button at his collar. "All the details haven't been worked out, but Hans has agreed to help with the project."

"I'd like to help, too." For several years, Constance had been in charge of growing the produce for her family. "I have a lot of experience."

"This is sounding better all the time." Mary smiled up at her husband.

When Constance saw the look of love Jackson gave his wife, she wondered if a man would ever look at her like that. She longed for it.

"One of the reasons I wanted to see if Hans would help is that I don't want Mary to do too much."

"It won't hurt me." She tapped his shoulder with a playful nudge. "We'd like the two of you to be the first to know. Sometime in late autumn, there is going to be an addition to the Reeves family."

Constance clapped her hands. "Oh, Mary, that's wonderful. Jackson is right. You shouldn't do too much. Let the three of us do most of the work."

"Along with other parishioners who want to help," Jackson added.

"Friday is usually a slow day at the smithy." Hans gazed out the back door at the property. "I'll come over and start plowing."

Jackson left his wife's side and leaned one hand against the doorpost. "I'll be free to help you. We should be able to put in at least a couple of acres or more. That will grow quite a few vegetables."

Constance turned to Mary. "Do you have a root cellar?"

"Of course."

"Then maybe you should plan on at least an acre of potatoes. They last a long time in a root cellar and can be used in so many ways."

Before Constance and Hans left that afternoon, the four of them had planned how to lay out most of the rows. Jackson and Hans decided to call their undertaking the Community Garden.

When Hans arrived at the boardinghouse for supper the next day, his mind was full of all the plans they had made. Without hesitating, he told the others around the table about what was going on. Thomas and Theodore asked a number of intelligent questions about the undertaking.

"I, for one," Theodore said, "would like to help with this garden. We always had a large one when we were growing up, didn't we, brother?"

When Thomas nodded, his fringe of hair bobbed. "That's one of the things I miss by living in the boardinghouse in town. I really like to work in merchandising, and someday, I hope to own my own store, but I do miss the feeling of fresh-turned earth between my fingers." He got a faraway look in his eyes.

Hans would have never guessed. These brothers dressed like businessmen and talked a lot about their work. "We can use all the help we can get. The plot contains several acres."

Theodore turned toward Mrs. Barker. "How would you like to have fresh produce all summer?"

A big smile spread across her face. "If we have too much to use, I could always can some for the winter. Then our meals would be more than meat and potatoes in the coldest months."

Soon conversation buzzed around the table. Hans leaned back in his chair, enjoying all the fuss. This idea fueled so much interest, the group took on the feel of a real family.

"Mr. Van de Kieft." Martha Sutter leaned around Constance. "Do you think I could let my older students help with the project? Some of them live on farms, but many live in town. It would be good experience for them."

Hans turned his attention toward Constance. "What do you think?"

She cupped her chin with one hand. "What a wonderful idea! With so many people helping, maybe Mary won't feel that she has to do too much."

Hans nodded, wishing he could touch her chin the same way. "I'm going to start plowing next Friday."

"I'm usually off on Fridays." Thomas looked at his brother. "I'll help with the plowing. Maybe my brother can help us with the seeds."

"Consider it done." A pleased expression

stole over Theodore's usually solemn face.

Sylvia wasn't very talkative, but she chimed in, "I can help when you start planting. Just let me know."

Mrs. Barker got up to start serving the angel food cake Hans had been eyeing ever since he sat down. "It looks as if you have almost a full crew just waiting to help you, Hans."

"I'm sure Jackson will be glad for so many willing hands." The piece of cake she set in front of him had to be six inches high. The man who married Constance would be blessed indeed. For some reason, that thought didn't set too well with all the food he had eaten.

Work on the garden progressed at a fast pace. Constance helped all she could, but Pastor Jackson had asked her to try to keep Mary occupied in pursuits that weren't too strenuous. That wasn't an easy task. Mary often insisted that the work helped her gain strength she'd need to deliver the baby.

Constance was so caught up in the baking at the boardinghouse and working with Mary that she didn't think very often about her promise to her father. About a month after she came to Browning City, she and Mary were in the parlor of the parsonage, working on tiny clothing for the baby. Constance had hemmed a flannel blanket, and now she was crocheting an edging around it. A knock sounded at the door.

"You stay there," she said to Mary. "I'll see who it is."

Hans stood in the late afternoon sunlight that slanted onto the porch. Golden rays highlighted his hair and deepened the intensity of his blue eyes. He held his hat in his hands.

"Come in, Hans." She stepped back, and he entered.

"Don't get up, Mary. I came to see Constance."

Constance noticed that Mary had a satisfied look on her face just before she bent to make more tiny stitches in the gown she worked on.

"So what can I do for you, Hans?"

He put his hat under one arm and reached toward his shirt pocket with the other. "When I went to the post office to check for my mail, the postmaster asked me if I would give you this." He pulled out a slightly wrinkled, smudged letter.

"I wonder who that's from." The only person who had ever written to Constance had been Patience, but she couldn't know that Constance was in Iowa.

Hans grinned. "Open it and see." He didn't seem to be in any hurry to leave.

Constance dropped onto the sofa and studied the missive, turning it over and over. The words written on the outside were her name and General Delivery, Browning City, Iowa. The only people she had told where she was going were their closest neighbors. Bertram and Molly Smith had helped her get through the death of her mother and then the death of her father. She had thanked God for their presence in her life.

Hans still stood in the doorway to the entry hall. "Are you going to open it or not?" He sounded like a child who couldn't wait to open Christmas or birthday presents.

She turned it over, released the sealing wax, and spread the page flat. She knew the Smiths didn't have a lot of schooling, just the elementary grades available in their holler. There weren't many from that area who went as far in school as she had.

The writing looked spidery, but she was able to make out the words:

Constance,
  We don't know if'n yore coming back to yore home place or not. If yore not, would ya consider sellin it to me.

Constance glanced down to the bottom of the page to be sure it was written by Bertram. It was.

I been savin money hopin to get more land. If'n yore willin, I could pay ya a fair price.

When she saw the figure he had written as a fair price, she could hardly believe it. The amount was more money than she had ever dreamed of owning at one time. With that much, she could live comfortably for quite a while.

"Is it bad news, Constance?"

She glanced up at Hans. While she had been reading the letter, he had taken the chair across from her. She could feel his intent stare as if it were a physical touch.

"No." She let the hand holding the letter fall into her lap. "I wouldn't call it bad news. I just don't know what to think about it."

"Is it something you want to share with us?" Mary didn't take her eyes off of her sewing. "You don't have to if you don't want to."

Constance glanced from one to the other. "You two and Jackson are my best friends here, so I don't mind telling you. Maybe you can pray for me to know what to do."

After picking the letter back up, she read it to them.

When she mentioned the money, Hans widened his eyes at the amount, so she asked, "Do you think that's fair?"

He stood and paced across the room, turning his hat in his hands. "I don't know anything about your property. That would buy a pretty good farm around here . . . but do you really want to sell?"

"I don't know what I want to do." She folded the paper in half several times, then thrust it into the pocket of her skirt. "Bertram and Molly are looking out for things while I'm gone. I know that when — if I go back, I'll have to hire someone to help me. I can't do everything by myself. I'm not sure I can afford to do that. There's a lot to think about."

Hans stopped his pacing and stared out between the front curtains at the waning light. "Have you ever thought about staying here in Iowa?"

He turned back and their gazes connected and held for a long moment. How could Constance answer his question? Just thinking about being here with her new friends, including the man who stood across the room from her, brought happiness to her heart. Maybe mostly because of him. She couldn't tell him that.

"I like it here, and I feel an accepted part of the community, but I also have to fulfill my father's dying wish."

Constance noticed that even though Mary continued sewing, her gaze occasionally darted from one of them to the other. "So, Mary, what do you think?"

Mary put her work in her lap. "I think you were right when you said that you needed prayer. When Jackson comes home, and it should be anytime now, we should seek the Lord about this."

Hans stood clutching his hat in one hand, staring at Constance. She felt his gaze again.

"That would be nice. However, I need to go to the boardinghouse and help Mrs. Barker with supper." Constance stood.

"Why don't you come back after supper? You come, too, Hans." Mary laid her sewing in the basket at her feet.

"Ja, I agree." Hans came back to stand beside Constance. "May I walk over there with you?"

After Constance and Mrs. Barker finished doing the dishes, Hans escorted Constance back to the parsonage. "So have you been thinking a lot about that offer in the letter?"

She nodded. "Have you?"

"Ja." He had thought of nothing else.

What would it mean if Constance sold her farm? Would she stay here in Iowa? Did he want her to? Of course he did, but was it God's will for her to stay? Hans wanted God's best for her, but he hoped that didn't include taking her away from Browning City. The thought of Constance getting back on the stage and riding it out of town caused a pain deep in his heart.

There were other things to consider. Even though Constance said he was one of her best friends, she was still keeping some secret from him. In her busyness, she had stopped talking about the promise and finding Jim Mitchell, but today the letter had brought the issue to the forefront again. His heart told him he could trust her, but his mind couldn't get past the fact that she might be hiding something bad from him. Because of the way she had thrown herself into the life of the town, he couldn't imagine her wanting to find Jim Mitchell to marry him. There had to be something else. But what could it be? Maybe she would tell them tonight.

After the four of them had prayed for a while, Constance remembered the Scripture from the first message she had heard Jackson preach. Something about the secret things belonging to the Lord. That night when she was alone in her room, she walked to the window and looked out at the spring night. All kinds of plants and trees wore the splendor of their spring renewal. That splendor had been hidden through the winter, kept by God, awaiting the time to reemerge. Maybe the things in her life were like that, too. Was God keeping some things secret, waiting until the right time to reveal them to her?

Dear God, is there a reason Thou hast not helped me find Jim Mitchell? Is the time not right? I wish Thou still talked to people today. Is my new home supposed to be in Browning City away from the place where I experienced so much grief?

She pulled from her pocket the letter Bertram and Molly sent. After going over to the bureau, she spread the paper in the light from the candle. She traced each word with her finger. When she came to the amount of money, her finger tingled almost as if the numbers were alive. *Am I supposed to accept this offer?*

In the early morning light, she took out the unused paper, quill, and ink she had bought when she moved into the boarding-house. Carefully, she dipped the nib into the black liquid and spread her answer across the parchment. Then she dripped blood-red sealing wax to seal the message. After breakfast, she would post it.

EIGHT

Constance threw herself into working in the Community Garden. Doing the things she grew up with made her feel like a productive part of the town. After baking in the morning, then having a noon meal at the boardinghouse, she spent most of each afternoon either in the garden or with Mary.

Spring in Iowa was different from spring in the Ozarks but just as beautiful. Sunshine coaxed flowers to peek through partially opened buds. Robins hopped along the ground searching for worms. They and other birds were particularly fond of the soil Hans had turned over for the garden plot. As leaves began to fill the branches of nearby trees, the twittering of birds building nests lent a special musical background to the work. Constance hummed along with them while she pulled the weeds trying to grow between the rows.

Some days, several other people joined her

in her toil. When Hans was one of them, she liked to watch him out of the corners of her eyes. His well-developed muscles rippled as he worked with a hoe or planted another row. She wondered how his shirt kept from ripping, he filled it out so well.

That thought brought a blush. She felt the warmth creep up her neck and onto her cheeks. Hopefully, if anyone noticed, they would just think it was the sunshine giving her the rosy cheeks. She quickly averted her gaze and kept her head down.

One day, she decided it surely had been enough time to receive an answer from the letter she had sent the Smiths back in Arkansas. When she arrived at the post office, several other people stood in line to pick up mail. She had to wait her turn to talk to the postmaster.

She took her place behind a man she had never seen before. When he reached the front of the line, he and the postmaster started a long conversation. Since she was the last person in line, she wandered around the room, looking at various notices tacked up on the walls. Anything to make the wait more bearable.

The man talked really loudly, and one word stuck out to Constance. He said the name Mitchell. She started back across the room to ask him if he was kin to them, but he continued talking, and she could hear every word.

"It's too bad about those boys. I think they just lost their way after their parents died."

The postmaster nodded his agreement.

Constance couldn't hold in her curiosity any longer. "Excuse me, sir. Were you talking about Jim Mitchell by any chance?"

The man turned toward her and nodded, his scraggly beard bobbing up and down in rhythm with his head. "Yep. Him and his brother."

"I've been trying to find Jim Mitchell. He and my father were in the war together." She tried not to sound too eager.

"Well, I was just telling Hiram here" — he gestured toward the man behind the desk — "that both those boys got in a gunfight in a saloon north of here, and it didn't end good for them. They both died from their wounds."

Shock robbed Constance of speech for a moment. Jim Mitchell was dead. If that was true, she would be released from her promise, wouldn't she? But what about the gold?

"Where did you say this happened?" She stared up into the man's face, trying not to show him how interested she was in his answer.

He scratched his cheek through the beard. "Let me see. I think it was at Camden Junction. It's about a five-hour ride north of Browning City. I heard tell they are both buried there. Seems like they were the end of the line for the Mitchell family in these parts. It's just too bad. I always did like their parents."

Camden Junction. Constance would have to find out where that town was located. Maybe she could go there and be sure this man knew what he was talking about.

After finding out that she didn't have any mail, Constance walked slowly back to the boardinghouse. What did all this information mean to her? How she wished that God would talk to people today. She wanted to ask Him what she should do about all that was happening in her life.

That gold had to be somewhere. Maybe it was on the farm. Tomorrow after she finished baking, she would go out there and see for herself. She knew Martha planned to take her students to work in the garden, so no one would miss her.

All the time she worked in the garden that afternoon, she wanted to tell Mary what was going on, but she didn't want to worry her.

Maybe if Constance found the gold and gave it back to the government, then she would feel released from her promise to her pa. No one needed to know what Jim Mitchell did. She didn't want to give his family a bad name now that he was gone . . . if he really was.

The next day, she started baking earlier than usual. By the time Mrs. Barker got to the kitchen, Constance had a couple of pans of biscuits all ready for breakfast. She had started making double the amount of bread every other day, so she wouldn't need to bake bread today. There was enough left from yesterday's baking. By the time Mrs. Barker had breakfast ready, Constance had enough pies made to last through supper.

"You really are in a hurry." At least Mrs. Barker didn't sound upset. "Do you have special plans for today?"

"I just thought I would spend some time looking around the countryside today. Maybe I have spring fever." Constance kept her eyes on her work.

"You know, Constance, if you want to take a day off from the baking, it would be okay. You do more than your share of the work around here as it is." Mrs. Barker came over and gave Constance a quick hug.

Tears sprang to Constance's eyes. Mrs.

Barker made her feel more like a family member than an employee and boarder.

When she finished helping clean up the kitchen, she went by to see Mary. After they visited a few minutes, Constance told her that she wanted to explore the area for a while. Mary didn't seem concerned, so Constance soon left. She walked to the livery stable, being careful not to go by the smithy on the way. When she stepped into the large shadowed barn, an older man came out of one of the stalls.

"Can I help you, miss?" The man leaned his pitchfork against the wooden rails.

"I'd like to rent a horse." Constance tried not to look nervous, even though the anticipation of maybe finding something today made her almost quiver.

The man looked her up and down, but not in a bad way. "Have you ever ridden before?" He must have been sizing up her abilities. He probably didn't want an inexperienced rider to hurt one of his animals.

"Yes, we had a horse when I was growing up. I used to ride it across the mountain to school."

He stood with his hands on his hips. "So it's been awhile?"

"At least two or three years." Constance didn't like being put on the spot like that.

Why couldn't the man just rent her a horse and quit asking questions?

He went into the open tack room and took a bridle off a hook on the far wall. He turned and strode down to a stall at the other end of the structure. After opening the gate, he went in and put the harness on the animal, then led the horse toward her.

"This here horse is gentle but has enough spirit to make your ride a good one."

"Thank you, Mr . . . ?"

"Jones. Charlie Jones."

She took his proffered hand and shook it. "I'm Constance Miller. I'd like to rent the horse for most of the day. Should I pay you now?" She had some money tucked inside the waistband of her riding shirt. She'd find a way to remove it privately when she needed to.

"Naw. We can settle up when you get back." Charlie rubbed the horse's neck and gave it an affectionate pat.

He went through the open tack room doorway and brought out a side saddle. Constance hadn't ever seen one. She had just read about them. They sure looked different.

"I don't know how to use one of those." Constance pulled on the sides of her split skirt. "I've always ridden straddling the horse."

She watched Mr. Jones go back and exchange the saddle. He hefted it up on the back of the animal that stood patiently waiting.

"What's the horse's name?"

"Blaze, but it's talking about this" — he pointed to the white slash down the horse's face — "not about how fast he runs." He chuckled at his own joke.

Even though Constance didn't think his words were that funny, she laughed. She didn't want to insult the livery manager. After using the mounting block to get up on the horse's back, she turned him toward the street and started riding east. It didn't take her long to get a feel for the animal, and soon she was moving along at a good pace.

Hans headed toward the livery stable with some harness he had mended for Charlie. In his pocket, he carried a shriveled apple from his root cellar. He liked to give Blaze a special treat when he went by his stall. Maybe he'd take the horse out for a ride, since he didn't have much work right now.

"Charlie, I've got your harness." When Hans went from the bright sunlight into the shadows of the stable, for a moment he couldn't see anything. "Where are you?"

"Over here mucking out Blaze's stall."

Hans hung the harness on its usual hook before meandering down the length of the building. He leaned his forearms on the top rail of the enclosure and put one booted foot on the bottom rail. "So where is Blaze? I brought him a treat."

"I reckon you'll have to wait a bit before you give it to him." Charlie didn't let up working while he talked. "He probably won't be back for quite a while yet."

Hans dropped his foot back to the dirt floor. "Someone rent him for the day?"

Charlie stopped and peered intently at him. "Yup." He looked back down at the pile of soiled straw he'd pulled into the middle of the stall. "Some woman. Kind of pretty, but I don't think I've seen her before."

Hans straightened and shoved his hands into the back pockets of his trousers. "What did she look like?"

"I tole you she was pretty. A little bit of a thing, but she knew how to ride a horse." Charlie started forking the straw into his barrow.

"Did she have brown curly hair?"

"Don't know how curly it is, but her hair

was brown. She had it pulled back into her sun bonnet." He hefted another forkful into the conveyance.

"Did she tell you her name?" Hans hoped the thought that came into his mind was wrong.

"Yup. I don't let anyone take out a horse without leaving me their name. Constance Miller." Charlie leaned the pitchfork against the back wall of the stall and picked up the handles of the wooden wheelbarrow. "Anything else you need? I gotta go dump this mess."

"How long ago did she leave?"

Charlie stopped short and set the barrow down on its legs. "You sure do have a lot of questions this morning. Why do you want to know?"

"Miss Miller is a new friend of mine." Hans knew in his gut where Constance was going. Why didn't she ask him to go with her? Guess she hadn't believed him when he'd warned her about possible dangers out there. "I thought I might try to catch up with her. I'm not sure she understands all the dangers that could lurk outside town."

"Why didn't you say that right off?" Charlie started down the row of stalls, then stopped. "Blackie here is the fastest horse in this stable." He opened the gate, went in,

117

and closed it behind himself. "He's a little skittish, but you can handle him okay."

Hans started for the tack room to pick up the saddle he used when he rode. "You didn't tell me how long she's been gone."

"About half an hour, I reckon." Charlie led the horse toward Hans.

Hans made quick work of saddling Blackie. Then he leapt into the saddle and hightailed it down the road heading east out of town. He didn't want to ride the horse too hard, but anything could be going on out there. It wasn't often that renegade former soldiers or other highwaymen roamed this road, but it could happen at any time . . . even today.

When Constance left the edge of town, she urged the horse into a gallop but soon slowed down. The countryside spread around her with an abundance of grass, trees, and wildflowers in a rainbow of colors. She wanted to enjoy all the glory of spring that surrounded her. Unlike her first time outside town when she felt as though the sky pressed down on her, she realized how comfortably the gentle rolling hillocks undulated across the landscape. The beauty of the land bubbled with life, and birds soared above the trees she passed occasionally. Small fluffy clouds rested against the robin's-egg-blue sky but didn't block out any of the sunlight.

Since the horse could move faster than a wagon, it shouldn't take as long to arrive at the farm, so she wasn't really in a big hurry. It felt good to be on the back of a horse, and it was easier to ride the road cut across this wide-open prairie instead of up and down mountainsides, where the animal had to pick its way between rocks and brush. She didn't have to watch where her horse stepped as closely here as she did back home.

Even though Constance saw farmhouses, they all sat far from the country road she traveled. A feeling of isolation and loneliness crept upon her. Then she remembered the warning Hans had given about the possibility of meeting outlaws out here. Why hadn't she thought of that before she left town? Maybe she should have asked him to come with her, but surely he was too busy.

Constance watched the shadows among the groves of trees she passed. Could someone be hiding there waiting for an unsuspecting traveler to come along? If so, the outlaw wouldn't get anything from her. She hadn't brought a handbag, and most of her money was hidden under the mattress in her room at the boardinghouse. She knew she should think about putting it in the bank, but she hadn't expected to stay in Browning City so long.

Blaze must have sensed her apprehension, because he became skittish, side-stepping a little. Constance had to concentrate on controlling the beast. Then she heard it. The sound of approaching hoofbeats. Her heart beat a loud thunder, and fear tasted metallic on her tongue. They were still a long way off. She glanced over her shoulder and saw a lone rider gaining on her. Should she turn off the roadway and hide? It was probably too late for that.

They had been riding so long that she didn't want to push Blaze any harder. What should she do? She hadn't seen a farmhouse for quite a while. If she came upon a lane leading to one, maybe she should take her chances there.

She ventured one last glance over her shoulder, trying to gauge how long it would be before the man overtook her.

The closer Hans got to the rider up ahead, the more certain he was that it was Constance. It hadn't taken as long to catch up to her as he had feared it would. Hopefully, she wouldn't resent him for coming after her. For some reason, he felt as though he had to protect her — from harm and from herself.

Remembering those moments in Jackson and Mary's house when their gazes had connected and everything around them had dropped away, his heartbeat sped up to match the fast clip of the hoofbeats. Constance was wearing a dark brown riding skirt that flapped behind her in the wind. A green blouse and sunbonnet completed her outfit. Hans was sure the green flecks in her brown eyes would be prominent today. He imagined her smiling up into his eyes and almost lost his tight hold on the reins. He couldn't do that while they were traveling so fast.

Constance glanced back and seemed to speed up a little. Didn't she know who he was? Maybe not. She could be scared, thinking he was an outlaw. It served her right for not being more careful. If he thought she could hear him, he'd call out to her, but he was still too far away to make his words heard over the sound of two sets of pounding hoofbeats. He leaned over Blackie's neck.

When his attention returned to the rider up ahead, Hans felt his heart leap into his throat. Blaze had stepped into a rut or hole, and his right front leg gave way under him. He went down. With horror, he watched Constance roll with the animal before she let go of the reins and flew away from him. At least Blaze didn't land on top of her. If he had, he would have crushed her.

Knowing that it wasn't good for Blackie, Hans urged the horse to go even faster. What if Constance was hurt? His heart stopped beating for a second before rapidly returning to its fast cadence.

When they approached the spot where Constance lay, Hans pulled back too hard on the reins. He would have to apologize to Blackie later, but he had to make sure Constance was all right. He leapt from the horse's back and dropped the reins, knowing that Blackie wouldn't wander far from where he left him.

Constance was too still, and her face looked as white as the snow that had covered the countryside not too long before she arrived in Browning City. Her long eyelashes fanned across her cheeks in a dark brown smudge. Even her lips, which usually were a healthy pink, looked a strange bluish tint. *Oh God, please don't let her be dead.*

Hans dropped to his knees on the grassy verge beside her. A faint pulse beat at her throat, and her chest rose and fell in shallow breaths. What should he do now?

NINE

Constance floated in blackness, trying to find a tiny speck of light. No other sensation registered in her muddled brain. The sound of hoofbeats rapidly approaching caused her heartbeat to accelerate right along with them. She felt the pounding of each hoof beneath her. Would the horse run over her? And why would a horse be coming toward her when she was asleep?

She realized she wasn't in her bed. Instead she was lying on something hard. Constance rubbed the fingers of one hand against the surface, only moving a couple of inches. Grass . . . the ground beneath . . . a pebble or two. Where was she, and why couldn't she open her eyes? She tried to take a deep breath but could only grasp a shallow one.

The horse stopped short, and a man's voice whispered, "I'm sorry, Blackie."

She heard the animal's huffing breath and the warm earthy smell of lathery sweat. The man's voice sounded familiar. She couldn't quite remember why. Maybe if she lay really still and thought about it, the answer would come to her.

"Oh, Constance, what am I going to do now?"

Hans. At the whispered question, an image of his face swam into her mind. The fragrance of heat and masculinity that she associated with the blacksmith invaded her senses. She forced her eyes open a bit. He leaned over her, only a breath away. For a moment, the look of concern — and something else — in his eyes called to something deep inside her. Sensations she had never experienced surged through her, warring with unrest and unnamed pain.

When Constance's eyes fluttered open, Hans leaned back away from her, hunkering with his feet under him. Healthy color finally suffused her face, and her breathing sounded more normal.

"Are you injured?"

She stared up at him without saying a thing, so he sat down on the soft, green grass near her head and lifted it into his lap. The fall had knocked her bonnet off her head, but its ties held it against her back. All of the pins that usually held Constance's hair had scattered, so her curls spilled around her, setting off her lovely face.

His desire to run his fingers though the glistening softness made his hand tingle. Hans looked up at the sky and took a deep breath. He needed to concentrate on making sure Constance was all right. He would have to deal with his runaway emotions later.

"I don't think so." The whisper was almost softer than the breeze that cooled them.

Hans stared into her eyes, which had darkened to almost chocolate brown. He loved the myriad of colors that they exhibited. *Hazel.* He'd heard someone call that color of eyes hazel. Whatever shade they were, he could almost drown in them.

"I'm going to lay you back down. I want to check on your horse. Then we'll go back to town."

Constance felt bereft when he left her. Carefully, she eased into a sitting position. Her hair tumbled down to her waist, and finally, she could breathe easier. While being totally aware of Hans's every move, she glanced around, trying to find some of her hairpins. Mother had always told her that a lady wore her hair up instead of letting her curls riot down her back. She picked up all she could reach without moving too much. While she gathered her hair into some semblance of a bun, Constance watched Hans.

He approached Blaze, talking in a soothing tone. The horse shuffled over, favoring one front leg. Probably that was the reason they went down. She hoped he wasn't hurt too bad.

She glanced back and noticed a particularly deep rut cut crossways in the road. She should have watched where they were going instead of urging the horse to go faster. They could have avoided the hole. Why hadn't she paid more attention to what she was doing?

Hans had gotten his hand on the bridle. He reached into one pocket, pulled out something, and held it under the horse's mouth. Blaze nipped the item and chewed contentedly, allowing Hans to check out his front leg.

"Is he going to be all right?" Constance pulled her bonnet back onto her head, hoping it would hold the hair in place long enough to get back home.

Home. The boardinghouse . . . and Browning City was beginning to feel like home to her. She was glad she had written to Bertram and Molly, telling them she would sell them the farm and having them send her all the personal items still left in the cabin. She didn't know if she would stay in Iowa, but she wanted the comfort of having a place where she felt safe and accepted, maybe even loved, by wonderful people.

Hans led Blaze over to the large black stallion he had been riding. He attached the reins to the back of his saddle and gave both horses a few loving pats before he turned back toward her. Anticipation poured through her as his long stride brought him closer.

Hans strode over to where Constance sat on the ground. She hadn't stood up, but she had tamed her hair. Too bad. He liked to see it tumble over her shoulders. The Bible was right when it called a woman's hair her glory, and Constance's had looked glorious spread across his lap awhile ago. He took his thoughts captive by the time he reached her.

"Let me help you up."

When he reached down, he placed his hands on either side of her waist and lifted her into a standing position. She trembled, and he pulled her into his arms . . . just to support her while she got her bearings, right?

"Do you hurt anywhere?"

"All over, I think." Her words spoken against his shirt brought warmth to his chest, inside and out.

He swept her up into his arms and walked toward Blackie, thankful that the horse was so powerful. Carrying two people shouldn't tax him too much.

"We'll have to ride together. I don't want to injure Blaze's leg any more than it already is."

Constance clung to his neck with both arms. "Will he be all right?"

"Yes." He stared straight ahead, not wanting to look down into her eyes, which were too close for comfort. "He just doesn't need to carry any extra weight back to town."

Hans swung Constance up onto Blackie's back, then mounted behind her. The ride to town would be exquisite torture, but he didn't mind. They would have to go slow because of Blaze's injury. Hans wanted to savor the feel of Constance in his arms for as long as it lasted. It might be the last time they would be that close.

Finding it hard to control his emotions, Hans studied the landscape around them. He should have gone riding sooner. Spring was his favorite time of year. Everything looked bright and fresh. It reminded him of the hope of renewal that the Lord gave every day. A profusion of colors spread around them, but he couldn't concentrate on any of them.

When he was near Constance, the fragrance of some flower floated around her. This close, it filled his senses. He had to get his mind onto something else.

"What in the world were you thinking, coming out here alone?" He knew he sounded harsh, but she needed to understand the risk she took.

She stiffened in his arms.

Why did men always think they were right? Constance gritted her teeth before she lashed out at him. After all, he had rescued her . . . again.

"I didn't think about it being dangerous."

"I'm sure you didn't." The steel in his tone cut like a knife. "Were you headed toward the Mitchell place?"

How did he know that? Could he read her mind? "Yes. I wanted to see if anyone had come home."

They rode in silence for a few minutes before he said anything else. She could feel the tension coiled like a tightly wound clock in the man behind her.

When he finally spoke, his tone wasn't as strident. "I would have come with you to keep you safe."

Of course, he would have. If he had come, she would have had to tell him more of her reasons for searching the house, and she didn't want to do that. At least not yet.

More of the muscles in her body began to announce their presence, aching and sore. Maybe she was hurt more than she thought. Riding on a horse for a long time didn't help.

"What is so important that you felt you had to go out there alone?"

The question hung unanswered between them. She wasn't going to tell him another thing.

As they continued to amble along, the rhythm of the ride lulled her, and soon she slumped against him. Even though his muscles were taut, they gave a welcome warmth and cushioned her exhaustion.

Hans knew the moment Constance fell asleep. He hoped she hadn't hit her head too hard. He knew that it wasn't good for a person to go to sleep so soon after a head injury. Hopefully, she was just tired.

He held the reins with one hand and pulled her closer with the other arm. Holding her cradled in his embrace felt somehow right. When he got home, he was going to have a long talk with the Lord about what to do about this woman.

When Hans stopped the horses outside the doctor's office, Constance stirred in his arms. He took one last moment to enjoy her essence before she was fully awake.

She stretched as she sat up away from him. "Where are we?"

"Dr. Harding's house." Hans slipped off the horse, then reached back for her.

"I don't need a doctor."

Hans helped her down, and when her feet reached the ground, her knees buckled. He held her up, then pulled her against him. "We've been on the horse a long time."

He was glad the doctor lived on the edge of town, and there weren't any people in sight. They might misconstrue why he was riding and holding her in his arms. He didn't want anything to sully her reputation.

Constance pulled back. "I can stand up."

"Are you sure? Let me help you inside."

This time, she didn't argue. They walked slowly, and she limped a little.

When Hans knocked on the door, the doctor answered. The older man took one look at Constance and stepped back, giving them plenty of room to enter. "So what happened?"

"She was thrown from a horse." Hans looked down at her and read the pain in her eyes. "I don't think she's hurt too bad, but we had a long ride back to town."

"Bring her into my exam room." Doc Harding led the way. "Did it knock her unconscious, young man?"

"Yes. She was just coming to when I reached her." Hans picked her up, and this time she didn't object.

While he was laying her on the bed in the examining room, Mrs. Harding bustled through the door.

"I'll take over now, young man, and my wife will assist me." The doctor was all business. "You can come back and check on her later."

Hans glanced at Constance, and she nodded. "I need to get the horses to the livery stable anyway. I will be back, though."

When Hans walked out of the room, Constance relaxed. Having him near kept her in a constant state of unrest. She didn't want to think about why.

"Let's have a look at you." The doctor, an older man with a shock of white hair and unruly brows over kind eyes, reminded her of one of her neighbors back home. "Where do you hurt?"

"All over, I think." She tried to laugh, but even that caused pain.

The doctor's wife took Constance's hand. "I'm Wilma Harding, and this old sawbones is my husband. He just wants to help you, but he'll have to examine you. Would it be all right if I help you out of these clothes and into a gown?"

Constance cut her eyes toward the tall man.

"I'll be waiting right outside until you ladies are finished."

When the door closed behind him, Constance let go of the breath she had been holding. Wilma Harding got a voluminous white gown from a chest beside the door. She helped Constance slip it over her head before she started removing her clothing under the covering. Constance was glad that she didn't have to undress completely in front of the woman.

Soon the doctor returned and started prodding various places on her body. "You already have some bruising. Did you land on your back?"

She nodded.

"Then you need to turn over."

After Constance settled on her stomach, Mrs. Harding put a soft pillow under her head. Then she took Constance's hand once again.

"I'm trying not to hurt you," the doctor explained, "but there must have been some rocks under you. A few of these bruises look like they go pretty deep. You're going to be sore for a while."

He straightened up, and Mrs. Harding helped Constance rearrange the gown.

"I don't think you have any broken bones." Dr. Harding stroked the white goatee on his chin. "Since you were unconscious for a bit, I want to keep you under observation for a while."

Constance tried to sit up. "But I have a job." Mrs. Harding gently pushed her back down on the bed. "I bake for Mrs. Barker."

The doctor stared at her for a minute. "Someone will let her know where you are."

While he rode Blackie to the livery stable on the other side of town, Hans prayed for the doctor to know how to help Constance.

Charlie stood in the open doorway of the stable with his thumbs tucked under his suspenders and watched Hans ride toward him. "What happened to Blaze, and where is Miss Miller?"

By the time Hans had dismounted, Charlie was examining the horse's front leg.

135

"Blaze stepped into a rut while going pretty fast. When he went down, Constance was thrown to the ground. I wasn't too far back down the road, so I helped them. I left her at Doc's."

Charlie nodded. "Good . . . good. I've got some liniment that should help this soreness. It shouldn't take too long for Blaze to be completely restored."

"If it's all right with you, I'll keep Blackie a while longer."

"Yup. Go right ahead." Charlie led Blaze into the stable.

With determination, Hans turned the horse around and rode away.

TEN

When the doctor finished with Constance, he asked his wife to stay with her. He didn't want Constance to go to sleep for a while since she hit her head when she fell.

Mrs. Harding sat beside the bed. A knitting basket rested on the floor beside her chair, and a mountain of something filled her lap. Her clicking needles punctuated the conversation.

Constance liked the woman. Her tender, helpful heart shone through everything she did.

"How long have you been in Browning City, Constance?" Mrs. Harding switched directions on the blanket or whatever it was going to be.

"More than a month." Constance wished she wasn't lying so flat. She would rather face the doctor's wife more comfortably. "Several weeks. I would have to count up to be sure." She looked all around the room, trying to see if there were any more pillows anywhere.

The knitting landed on the basket and spilled onto the floor. "Do you need something, dear?" Mrs. Harding leaned forward, and her kind eyes studied Constance's face.

"I just thought if I had more pillows, I would be more comfortable."

The other woman bustled back to the chest beside the door and pulled three puffy pillows from its depths. After placing them behind Constance's back, she sat down and picked up her work.

"Now, where were we?" The rhythm of stitches continued as if there hadn't been an interruption. "Where did you live before you came here?"

Constance knew the woman was trying to keep her occupied, but she wasn't sure she wanted to tell her every detail of her life. "I've always lived in the Ozark Mountains of Arkansas."

Before another question was forthcoming, thankfully, a knock sounded on the front door of the house.

"I'll be right back. Just don't go to sleep while I'm gone."

In her mind, Constance followed Mrs. Harding's footsteps up the hallway. She heard the front door unlatch and muffled voices carry on a conversation. The other woman's voice sounded vaguely familiar, but because the two women spoke so softly, she wasn't sure who exactly. Soon, two sets of footsteps came back down the hallway.

"Constance, look who came to check on you." Mrs. Harding preceded the visitor through the doorway.

"Mary." Constance was glad to see her friend. "How did you know I was here?"

The pastor's wife smiled at her. "Hans came to tell me. We agreed that you shouldn't go back to your room at the boardinghouse. I'm going to take you to the parsonage to recover. He should be here soon with a buggy." She turned toward the doctor's wife. "That is, if it's all right with you."

"I've enjoyed having her, but I do believe it would be better if she were with good friends." She picked up her knitting and moved it away from the chair. "Why don't you sit down and visit with Constance? I'll go get you some coffee."

Mary sank into the chair but put a restraining hand on Mrs. Harding's arm. "I don't need any coffee. Hans should be here soon."

Almost before Constance realized what was happening, she rested once again in the strong arms of the man who rescued her. Hans carried her out to the waiting carriage and placed her in the cushioned rear seat. Then he lifted Mary up to sit beside her.

He drove slowly toward the parsonage, probably to keep from jarring Constance too much. The man's thoughtfulness touched a place in her heart. No one had ever taken such good care of her. She was usually the one seeing to other people's needs.

Mary kept up a running commentary all during the ride. At the house, Hans lifted Mary down, and she proceeded up the walk to open the door.

When he lifted Constance from the vehicle, she started to tell him that she could walk. He didn't give her a chance, because he swept up the walk and into the house very quickly. Instead of taking her into a bedroom, he set her down in an overstuffed chair in the parlor.

"Thank you, Hans." Mary hovered near. "Why don't you come back and share supper with us? I'm sure Jackson will want to hear all about your exciting day."

Hans tipped his cap. "I'd be obliged." He turned to Constance. "I'll go tell Mrs. Barker what happened so she won't expect you back for a few days."

After he left, Constance exclaimed, "A few days? I should be okay by tomorrow."

Mary sat on the end of the sofa nearest her. "We don't want to rush it. It will be my pleasure to have you here."

"But you're going to have a baby. You shouldn't have to take care of me."

Mary laughed. "Oh, Constance, not you, too. Jackson acts as if I'm made of blown glass. I'm perfectly healthy, and I will love having you here with me for a few days."

When Hans returned for supper that evening, Constance still sat in the comfortable chair. He was glad to see that healthy color had returned to her face.

"Mary won't let me lift a finger. I could get spoiled if this continues." The twinkle in Constance's eyes went straight to his heart.

"I don't think you have to worry about that." He pulled a straight chair near hers. "I hope I didn't scare you when I rode toward you. Was that why you rode faster?"

Constance's gaze dropped to her hands, which she twisted in her lap. "I probably owe you an apology. I should have listened to you about the dangers of riding alone. When I heard you coming, I was afraid you were a highwayman."

She turned her eyes toward him, and her

expression held true remorse. "We both made a mistake. Let's just forgive each other."

"Ja, forgiveness is a good thing."

Supper with his three best friends loomed as a blessed promise. *Best friend? Is that all Constance is?* But she couldn't be anything else until she opened up to him completely. He had prayed about her often, and he felt that God wanted them to be together, at least for now. Even though they had spent a lot of time together, she still held something back.

He wasn't getting any younger, and he had asked God often enough to bring someone into his life for a lasting relationship, but there was no one else who interested him — not before Constance came to town, and especially not now.

After watching the happiness marriage brought to both Jackson and Mary, Hans wanted the same thing for himself: A woman who would be the helpmeet Scripture speaks about. A woman to share the same dreams and goals. A woman to be the mother of his children and who really wanted those children. He didn't even know if Constance liked being around young ones.

He turned his attention to the woman in question. "Do you have any brothers or sisters back home?"

Sadness fell like a veil over her face. "No. I'm an only child. If there had been anyone else, maybe Pa wouldn't have sent me on this quest."

Perhaps he had misjudged exactly why she was looking for Jim Mitchell. If she were going to marry the man, she wouldn't have said that, would she?

"When you marry, are you looking forward to having children, Constance?"

She narrowed her eyes in a thoughtful faraway look before answering. "I hope God gives me lots of children. I didn't like being an only child." She turned a dazzling smile toward him. "Hans, why all the interest in my future?"

Since he couldn't think of how to answer that, he was glad that Mary called them to supper.

Finally Constance was back at the boardinghouse. When she made her way to the kitchen that morning, Mrs. Barker expressed gratitude for having her back. While Constance worked, her thoughts returned to the last few days. She hadn't planned on staying at the parsonage for more than a week, but until yesterday, each time she expressed a desire to go home, Mary had discouraged her.

Hans had spent a lot of time with her. She liked him, but when he was in the room with her, something inside her felt agitated . . . or more alive. She wasn't sure which. She wondered if he didn't have much work at the smithy. He was always underfoot. Probably since she had resumed her job, he would only come by at suppertime.

Constance felt as if she were in some kind of suspension, not able to make plans until she could fulfill her promise to her father. She even tried to talk to God about it, but He seemed so far away. Her questions about why He had taken her ma and pa hit the ceiling and bounced back. She had even asked Him to help her find Jim Mitchell, but that prayer also didn't seem to reach heaven.

Maybe she should just continue with the search herself. The sooner, the better.

A few days later after she had made an extra supply of baked goods, she told Mrs. Barker that she wanted to take the next day off.

Early in the morning, she ate her breakfast, wrapped leftover biscuits and bacon in a rag, and set out for the livery stable. She knew Hans wouldn't like her going off by herself, but she had to finish this before she could move on with her life. After all, the man wasn't her keeper.

Hans enjoyed the freedom of being able to see Constance so often when she was at the parsonage. After she went back to work at the boardinghouse, he had to catch up with his work, but each evening at supper, he worked the conversation with Constance around to what she was going to do the next day. If she said she was going anywhere, he kept an eye out for her, trying not to let her know that he was watching her. Somehow, he knew she wouldn't appreciate it. That woman needed a keeper . . . or protector, and he was just the man to do it, whether she agreed or not.

Last night, Constance had seemed evasive when they were talking. Something was up, and he figured it had to do with going back out to the Mitchell farm. He went to the livery early and rented Blackie for the day. By the time she came, rented Blaze, and started on the road toward the farm, he was already on the way. But he went across country, from one copse of trees to the next, never getting very far from the road.

Sure enough, Constance galloped down the road not long after he left town. He kept far enough away so she didn't see him, but he was careful not to let her completely out of his sight. Soon she slowed to a comfortable pace. As he watched her, she seemed to be taking the time to enjoy the countryside, but she headed straight down the road toward the farm.

Hans would like to enjoy the surroundings, but he didn't want to take the chance that she was really going somewhere else. He kept his attention on her.

Constance rode directly up to the house. She dismounted beside the front porch and tied Blaze's reins to one of the supporting columns.

Hans dismounted far enough away so Constance couldn't hear him approach. While he led Blackie, Hans watched her knock on the door. After a short time, she tried the door, opened it, and walked in. He picked up his pace, hoping she wouldn't hear him.

A loud shriek accompanied a crashing sound that came from inside the house. Hans jumped on Blackie's back and urged him into a run. When he was almost at the house, he jumped out of the saddle and hit the ground running. His footsteps pounded up the steps and across the porch.

■ ■ ■ ■

When Hans burst through the door, Constance could hardly believe her eyes. What was he doing here? And why did he have to come at just that moment? She must look awful.

She had been walking across the room when the floorboards gave way with a crash. They were rotten and couldn't hold her weight. She had feared she was going to fall a long way. Instead, the root cellar was shallow, so when she fell, her head remained above the floor. She didn't even want to look at Hans, knowing that she was surrounded by a cloud of dust and splintered wood. She was afraid to move too much, because some of the sharp boards could pierce her body.

"Constance, what have you done?" His shout made her angry.

"What have I done? What are you doing here?" She tried to put her hands on her hips, but shards of wood scraped her wrists. She burst into tears.

Shock and confusion covered his face. "I'm going to help you, Constance. Don't move until I get there."

With both arms out as if to break a fall if

it came, Hans walked toward her, testing the floor boards as he came.

The sight that had greeted Hans when he burst through the door brought the upheaval of an earthquake to his emotions. Constance had been covered with dust. Only the whites of her eyes stood out from the dirty color that cloaked her from the top of her head all the way down as far as he could see of her in between broken boards. The jagged wood that reached toward her looked like menacing arms of death. He whispered a quick prayer for her safety and his own wisdom.

He shouldn't have yelled at her. It was a reaction he hadn't been able to tame. Now he must help her, and to make matters worse, she had started sobbing.

"Please don't cry." He tried to sound soothing. "I'm going to get you out of there."

Most of the boards that made up the floor of the room were all right. Just the few down the center had been weak.

"Look at me, Constance." His stare willed her to turn her gaze toward him.

When she finally did, the despair he saw almost brought him to his knees.

"You need to trust me completely. Don't

move until I tell you to, and only move in the direction I say. Okay?"

She finally gave a slight nod, fear from her gaze spearing through him.

"I'm going to pull this board up." He indicated which one. "Please don't move toward it in any way."

"Okay." Her whisper resounded through the silent room.

He gingerly worked with the board, pulling it away from her body, then ripped it out and threw it to one side of the room. It landed with a thunk and a cloud of dust against the wall. One board on each side of it needed to come out before he could rescue her. Taking great care, he pulled each one out. Moving carefully, he scooted near the edge and reached for her.

Hans grasped her wrist. "It would help if you held on to my wrist, too."

Constance turned her arms until she could latch onto his. They tightened their interlocked grips, and he pulled her up. When she stood on both her feet, she pulled from his hold and started trying to brush her clothes with her hands.

He grabbed her arms to stop her. "Constance, it won't do any good. Look how much debris is clinging to your skirt."

"Eew." She made a face. "I don't like bugs

on me."

In among the dust that layered her clothing, he saw cobwebs and insects clinging in clumps. "Let's get you outside and see what we can accomplish together."

Docilely, she followed him. Hans was glad she hadn't argued. Maybe this wasn't as bad as it seemed.

"If I break a branch off of a bush, we can use it to brush you off." He jumped off the porch and headed toward the nearest thicket.

When he returned, she stood in the grass not far from the porch. He started brushing her below the waist in the back. She turned slowly allowing him access to her whole skirt. Meanwhile, she used her hands on the front of her bodice. He could brush off her back.

After they finished, he noticed the tracks of tears on her dirty cheeks. He pulled a bandanna from his back pocket. "You might want to use this to wipe your face."

She swiped it up one side and down the other, smearing more than removing the dirt. He didn't want to point it out to her, because she didn't seem to be in a very good mood. Who could blame her? But it was her own fault.

"Constance, what were you thinking?" His

harshness should show her just how foolish her actions had been.

Instead, all his words did was inflame her anger. "What were you doing following me?" Her hands fisted on her hips, and she glared from behind the dirt masking her face.

"Didn't you learn your lesson the last time you rode out alone?" He knew his tone was even louder, but the woman wasn't listening to his good advice.

"I am an adult. I don't need a keeper." Her volume grew to match his.

Two could play the same game. He placed his fists on his own hips. "Yes, you do. What would you have done if I hadn't followed you? You couldn't have gotten out of there without hurting yourself more." What he wanted to do was shake some sense into her.

He reached for her arms, and she burst into great heaving sobs. Hans pulled her toward him and cradled her against his chest. *Lord, what am I going to do with Constance?*

Eleven

The bell over the door of the mercantile jingled, alerting Constance that someone else had entered the store. She glanced toward the front and sighed. Hans stood so tall and broad-shouldered that he blocked out most of the light from the glass in the door. She fought against her own heart. Just the sight of the man caused it to flutter in her chest of its own accord. She took a breath, trying to calm down. Yes, he was handsome. Yes, she enjoyed spending time in his company. But the man had become her shadow. Wherever she went, he went.

She moved down the aisle and stopped to finger a roll of lace. The intricate creamy pattern would look good decorating the collar of the brown dress she had on today. The frippery didn't hold her attention long. From across the room, she felt every move the man made. Probably she shouldn't touch any more fabric because her palms were beginning to sweat. What was wrong with her?

Granted, Hans had rescued her a few times, and she was thankful for that. More than thankful, really. What would she have done if he hadn't come along? She shuddered to think about it. Somehow he had decided that she needed a keeper, and he was the man for the job.

Constance turned to walk between other counters containing a myriad of products. Up ahead, she spied shiny new shovels leaning against the back wall, and an idea took root in her mind. The gold had to be somewhere. Perhaps Jim Mitchell had buried it on the farm. She could use a spade like that to try to dig up the treasure.

She didn't want to alert Hans to what she was thinking, so she turned to look at the candy sticks. Constance was partial to peppermint. She also liked horehound. Her mother had used them to help when Constance had a cough, but she never felt as if they were medicine. She could almost taste them now, and a craving took up residence in her mouth.

After choosing two of each of the sugary confections, she pulled her coin purse from her reticule. While she finished paying the clerk, Hans stopped beside her. She could feel his heat, even though he was at least a foot away from her.

When the other man went to help another customer, Hans leaned one hand on the counter. "Good to see you, Constance. So you have a sweet tooth."

She held one of the sticks toward him. "Would you like one?"

He smiled, never taking his eyes from her face, as his hand closed around her fingers. "You don't have to buy me one."

"I know I don't." She tried to turn on all her charm. "I just wanted to be nice."

"Thank you." He still held her fingertips along with the candy. He pulled it to his lips and bit a chunk off the end. The crunch sounded almost as loud as her thudding heartbeat.

The gesture seemed much too intimate for a public store. Constance hoped no one watched them. Heat stole its way into her cheeks.

Hans took the candy from her with his other hand, not letting go of her fingertips. For a moment, the world around them melted into nothingness. Constance was held captive in his warm gaze, and the room seemed to empty of air. She gulped a shallow breath, and he slowly released his hold on her.

"See you at supper tonight." He turned and sauntered away as if nothing had happened.

How could he? Everything in her world had shifted, and he apparently didn't feel a thing. She watched him walk out the door.

She turned and stalked to the shovels. The sooner she fulfilled her promise, the better. Her life had just become much too complicated. Maybe she should leave this place as soon as possible.

What was I thinking? Hans berated himself as he hurried toward the smithy. The exchange with Constance had quickly escalated into something where he was no longer in control.

Lord, what am I going to do? The woman . . . Constance does things to me that I don't understand. Should I keep my distance until she is honest with me? But, Lord, she needs a protector. No telling what she would do without someone to rescue her. Why do I feel so drawn to her?

At least the store was a very public place. The desire to pull her into his arms and kiss her had almost overwhelmed him. That's why he had turned and run. Why had he gone to the store? Right. He needed to pick up some things Evan Cooper, the owner, needed repaired. Now he would have to make another trip, but not while Constance was still in there. How much control could one man have?

He knew she needed protecting, but he would have to keep more distance between them. She hadn't been out of town for a couple of weeks, and nothing had happened to her. Maybe he could relax a little, let her get on with her life. She hadn't done anything to make him think she would try striking out alone again. When he saw her at supper each night, her happiness and contentment radiated through the room.

He figured that she had almost forgotten about the reason she came to Iowa, and he felt sure her letter had told those neighbors back home that she would be making her home in Browning City for now. Whistling as he walked, he returned to the smithy in time for the livery owner to bring in three horses for shoeing.

Constance glanced down the street toward the smithy. Hans was out front shoeing a horse. Since he hadn't been back long, he should be occupied for a while. She needed to test out her theory that the gold was buried on the farm.

She hurried to the boardinghouse and put

on her riding clothes. After stopping in the kitchen to tell Mrs. Barker that she would be gone most of the day, she headed to the livery. Soon she rode Blaze back to the boardinghouse to get a large tow sack that contained the shovel and a rope. She hadn't wanted to take them to the livery with her because Charlie might notice and ask questions.

Feeling at one with the horse, she spent the ride to the farm in a pleasant lope. After she arrived, she led him to the spring quite a ways into the woods behind the house. Constance tied the rope to a small tree, giving the horse plenty of room to graze and reach the water when he was thirsty. Taking the shovel and sack, she went back to the front porch, where she sat down on the edge and glanced around.

If I were a man, where would I hide the gold? There were plenty of places. Would Jim Mitchell have wanted to keep it hidden from his parents and even his brother? Maybe he would bury it in the edge of the woods behind the house. She left the sack on the porch and walked around the building, carrying the shovel.

It had rained often this spring, bringing forth a multitude of plants and flowers. That also helped keep the ground from being so hard. The loamy soil under the trees turned easily. She dug at the base of one tree then another. When she didn't hit a strongbox very soon, she moved on to other trees.

Dirt streaked her hands and arms, and the work caused sweat to pop out on her brow. She swiped it away with her forearm, then noticed the muddy smear on her arm where she had pushed up the sleeve when she first felt the heat. Probably there was one on her face, too. At least no one would see her like this. She went back to the spring and knelt on a rock ledge beside the pool. She reached into the cold water and rinsed her hands and arms before splashing some on her face.

Why didn't she wait until she had a drink before she did that? Now the water in front of her was dirty. Constance moved along the side until she came to a spot where the water was clear and clean before she cupped her hands to bring the soothing liquid to her mouth. Most of it drained between her fingers. She stooped farther down, with her face almost at the surface of the pool and tried again, hoping she wouldn't lose her balance and fall in. As wetness trickled down her throat, the cool liquid soothed her thirst.

"So, Blaze, are you enjoying your rest?"

Constance walked over to the horse and patted his neck.

The shadows thrown by the trees around her gave her a lonely feeling. If only she could find the gold soon and be on her way.

She returned to the clearing that contained the house. Maybe he hid it in the root cellar. After the fiasco of the last time she had entered the house, she didn't look forward to going in there again. But she had watched the way Hans carefully tried out each board before he put his full weight on it. She could do that.

After taking a deep, fortifying breath, Constance walked into the dim interior. She tested every board that was left in the floor of the main room. None of them gave way. The trapdoor to the cellar was in one corner of the room, near a window. She pulled back the curtains, and sunlight streamed through the space, highlighting the hole in the floor. She lifted the trapdoor and placed a tentative foot on the steps cut into the rock supporting the house.

Constance tiptoed down and bent her head so she could move around. She felt like an old woman the way she had to walk. She plunged the long shovel straight down into the dirt over and over, trying to find the treasure. The only hard thing she hit was the rock foundation.

When her back ached so much that she couldn't stand it another minute, she went back to the opening and climbed out. After letting the trapdoor down over the hole, she turned around in the sunlight. *What a mess!* Dirt covered every inch that she could see of herself. She felt sure there were no clean spots on the part she couldn't see either.

Now what should she do? Maybe Jim Mitchell hid it in front of the house. After hiking the shovel onto her shoulder, she went back outside and started to work. She turned over some dirt, pushed the shovel deeper into the soil several times, then moved on to another place. Methodically, she made her way back and forth across the meadow.

When Constance finished, she hadn't found anything but rocks, roots, worms, and bugs. What a waste of time. If she had been back home with her father still alive, he would have made use of the worms and bugs to go fishing.

She went back to the porch and dropped to sit on the front edge. Where had Jim Mitchell hidden the gold?

She tried to figure out reasonable things that could have happened. Perhaps he had other men help him, and one of them hid the gold. Maybe they all wasted their ill-gotten gain in riotous living. She had heard that ungodly men often did that. Since she had done everything she could to try to fulfill her promise to her father, maybe it was time to give up and get on with her life.

Constance smiled at the last thought. What would getting on with her life entail? The question brought a familiar face into her mind. Sparkling blue eyes that had darkened almost to navy when they were last in the mercantile. The only blond hair that she had ever wanted to run her fingers through. That man was too disturbing for her peace of mind.

When he lifted her hand and took a bite of the stick of peppermint she held, for a moment she had thought he was going to kiss her fingertips. Just as quickly, she wanted him to, even though there may have been other people near them. She didn't know if there were because all of her attention concentrated on the tall, brawny man whose eyes haunted her dreams, whether she was sleeping or awake.

She relived his full lips closing around the candy, and Constance wondered what it would feel like to have them touching hers. When that thought entered her mind, she touched her fingers to her mouth, and a sigh escaped from her soul. These thoughts were too disturbing, so she jumped up and started toward the spring. She might as well clean up and prepare to ride Blaze back to town. After glancing around the clearing, she knew that she couldn't leave without filling in all those holes, but first she needed a cool drink of water.

What was I thinking? How often had Hans asked himself that question since Constance fell out of the stagecoach into his waiting arms? More times than he wanted to count. She was constantly in his thoughts, making a home for herself that he didn't want to disturb.

When Charlie came back to pick up his horses, he mentioned that Constance had rented Blaze for a ride. Now Hans raced down the road toward the Mitchell farm. He had become complacent, and Constance had just been biding her time. What was so important that she had to keep going out there and endangering her life? Was she looking for something? If so, what could it be?

Maybe her father had given Jim Mitchell something that he wanted Constance to retrieve. It made sense. Even though sometimes Hans had thought something wrong was going on, the explanation could be as simple as that. Why hadn't he trusted Constance? Given her a chance to tell him in her own time?

Hopefully, his haste wouldn't be needed, because she wasn't in any danger, but something pushed him on. For some reason, he felt that Constance needed him today. Surely it wasn't because she was in peril again.

When he approached the farmhouse, he slowed Blackie to a walk. Fresh tracks led toward the house, but when they turned off the dirt road, they were swallowed up in the thick grass. He looked up from the tracks and couldn't believe his eyes.

The meadow in front of the farmhouse was pockmarked by many places where someone had been digging. He walked Blackie between them, being careful to keep the horse from stepping in one of the holes. Even by the porch was evidence of more digging. At the bases of the trees on the edge of the woods that surrounded the meadow on three sides, holes looked like some kind of open wounds in the earth.

Hans dismounted and stepped up on the porch. The recesses of the house weren't as dark as they had been the last time he was there. He glanced around inside and noticed that some of the curtains had been pushed back so that sunlight poured into the room.

"Constance, are you here?" His words echoed in the empty space.

Through the hole in the floor, he noticed that someone had been digging in the cellar, too. After carefully making his way around the opening, he opened the two doors that led off the main room. Both of the other rooms looked undisturbed. All the furniture, as well as the floor, wore a heavy coat of dust.

Where can she be?

Outside once again, Hans took a deep breath and walked toward the edge of the cliff.

TWELVE

Before Constance tried to get all the dirt off her hands and face, she made an attempt to remove the soil from her clothing the way Hans had before. A branch from a nearby bush worked fine on the front and sides, but she couldn't reach the middle of her back. She must look a sight with most of her clothing freshened and a streak running down one side. She'd make a pretty good skunk, wouldn't she?

That thought introduced the idea that these woods could contain one of those notoriously malodorous creatures. Hadn't she heard somewhere that they were nocturnal animals? Hopefully, any that lived near here were. Being on the receiving end of a spray from one of the black-and-white-striped animals would completely ruin the day.

What about her problem with her clothing? Constance walked over to a sturdy tree and rubbed against it with her back. Maybe that would help some.

Since she had done everything she could to clean off her dress, she knelt beside the clear pool. She had been so preoccupied when she was here earlier that she hadn't noticed the abundance of smooth pebbles that lined the bottom. Varying shades of browns, black, and white — some with shiny specks — formed a beautiful mosaic created by nature. Constance dipped one fingertip into the water, and ripples spread in ever-widening circles.

Her life was like that. She had spent so many years settled into her home in the Ozarks, but now her life spread across two state lines. Who knew where it might lead? She hoped that she presented to the world as pleasing a picture as the rocks in the bottom of this spring.

Another picture whisked into her mind, blurring out the pool and bringing a catch to her breath. Scenes played one after the other. Hans catching her in his strong arms with a startled expression in his blue eyes. Hans working in the Community Garden, taut muscles rippling with the rhythm of his work. His white teeth sinking into the peppermint stick with his lips wrapping around it, barely missing her fingertips. These thoughts did nothing to cool off Constance from her previous labors. If only she had her folding fan that rested in the top drawer of the chest in her room at the boarding-house. She would put it to good use.

Constance shook the thoughts from her mind and concentrated on washing her hands, arms, and face. Then she pulled her sleeves back down and buttoned her cuffs.

She walked over to the grazing horse. "Blaze, it won't be long until we start back to Browning City."

As Constance approached the edge of the woods, she thought she heard a male voice. Were there other men? She only heard one. Who could that be? Did she need to hide from the man?

She carefully worked her way between the bushes and trees without making a sound. When she peered around the trunk of one of the last large trees between her and the meadow, she saw a man standing near the edge of the bluff. Immediately, she recognized his clothing and the way he stood proudly with his head flung back. The sunlight glinting on his hair gave his locks a golden glow. What was Hans doing here?

He hadn't noticed her, and he continued to talk with a loud voice. She wondered if he was calling to someone across the Mississippi. Surely the river was too wide for him to be heard, even though he was shouting. Then she heard him say, "Lord." She stealthily moved closer to the house until she could understand every word.

"Lord, what am I going to do about Constance? You know how I feel about her, but is it Your will for me to spend so much time with her? How can I keep her safe if she won't tell me the truth? What is she looking for, and why won't she let me help her? Lord, I need some answers from You, and I need them as soon as possible."

Hans stared at the patchwork of cultivated ground across the river. Some farmer over there had started his spring planting. Too bad no one was working this farm. This year's planting season would soon be over. He thrust his hands into the back pockets of his trousers. Trying to take his mind off Constance only worked for a few seconds.

"Help me here, Lord. I really need You."

The snapping of a twig cut into the silence at the end of his sentence. He whirled and stared straight into the face of the woman who caused him so much unrest.

For a moment, her eyes widened. "Hans," she called to him. "What are you doing here?"

He loped across the meadow, being careful not to step into any of the holes. "I could ask you the same question." He gestured toward one of the pockmarks. "Why have you been digging here?"

Constance heaved a deep sigh, seeming to consider how to answer. During the lull, he reached her side. He had to grip his hands into fists to keep from reaching out to her; then he thrust his fingers into his back pockets.

She stared at him a long moment before answering. "Come sit down on the porch with me. I'll feel more comfortable talking to you there." She turned and led the way.

After she sat, he dropped down onto the wooden porch but not too close to her. He wanted to keep his wits about himself, and being too near Constance would muddle his thoughts. "What are you going to talk about?"

She turned her head and stared off into the distance. "I know you've been really helpful to me. . . ."

After her words faded off, he waited. Surely she had more to say.

"I guess you want to know the real reason I'm looking for Jim Mitchell."

He nodded, then realized she couldn't see his movement from there. *"Ja."*

■ ■ ■ ■

How could Constance tell her story without Hans getting the wrong impression of her father? She was tired of hiding things from Hans. Maybe the absolute truth would be best in this circumstance. She turned to look at him, and his intense scrutiny almost crumbled her defenses.

"I told you that my father made me promise to find Jim Mitchell."

"*Ja.*" He nodded again. "I remember."

The way he said it, she felt that his memories contained more than her comment about the promise. What if he was also remembering the moment in the mercantile? Heat crept into her cheeks, so she turned back to study a flock of birds heading north in the intense blue sky.

"It's kind of a long story."

"I have plenty of time." His tone held finality.

Constance knew she would have to tell him everything, even if it meant that Hans wouldn't trust her . . . or like her . . . anymore. "My father was a good man. He came back from the war changed. I don't think he ever got over it before he died." She glanced back at Hans. He didn't look disgusted yet.

"Ja. I've seen other men who were affected by the fighting." Hans lifted a foot onto the edge of the porch and leaned an arm on his upraised knee.

"I didn't know about any of this until he was dying. That's when he extracted the promise from me."

Constance didn't know why it was so hard to talk about what happened. She should just blurt it out. She had spent enough time with Hans to know that he was an honorable man. He would understand. She studied his hand that hung in the air. Maybe not looking at his face would make it easier.

"While they were together in the fighting, my father worked out a plan to steal a gold shipment from the Union soldiers." After that sentence, she ventured a glance at his face.

Hans shifted until he could lean back against the post holding up the roof of the porch. "I heard about that shipment being stolen. Is that what you're looking for?"

Disappointment wrinkled his brow, and she winced.

"Yes, but not for the reason you're probably thinking. You see, my father didn't take part in the robbery. He was a Christian. He said the war made him forget for a while, but he couldn't go through with the plan, and he thought he had convinced Jim Mitchell not to do it, either."

A look of relief softened Hans's expression. "Then who stole the gold?"

Constance took a deep breath before she continued. "The only person with him when he planned the job was Jim Mitchell, and the robber or robbers carried it out just the way Pa planned it. He was sure Mr. Mitchell did it."

"And he wanted you to come get his share." Now disgust colored his tone.

"No!" She was sure he would never believe her, but she might just as well finish the story. "Pa wanted me to tell Mr. Mitchell to give back the gold. Pa had been saving money so he would have enough to travel here and talk to him, but then Pa got sick. Just before he died, he told me where his savings were hidden and made me promise to convince his old friend to do the right thing. I never knew it would be so hard to fulfill that promise."

After she finished, she sat with her hands clasped in her lap, waiting for his comment, certain this admission would drive Hans away. Why would he want to protect her now? He evidently thought she was part of the whole bad mess.

"So all these holes were looking for the gold." His statement of the fact sounded almost like a question.

Constance nodded, not even turning her head. "I thought if I could find it and give it back to the government, I would have fulfilled the promise to my father."

Hans stood and moved in front of her. "Look at me, Constance."

She complied. With the bright sunlight behind him, she couldn't read his expression.

"None of this is your fault. You shouldn't have had to shoulder the burden alone." He reached out and took her hand in his. "I wish you had told me before. I could have helped you decide what to do."

With a tug of his hand, he pulled her to stand in front of him. Too close in front of him for her comfort.

"So what do I do now?"

Her question shook him. So did her inquiring gaze. As a man, he wanted to be able to fix everything for her, but how could he take care of all this? Where should he start?

"First let's get these holes filled. I'll help you." He glanced around the clearing, feeling more in control since there was something tangible to accomplish. "Where is the

173

shovel you used?"

"Down by the spring." For the first time in weeks, her heart felt lighter. "That's where I have Blaze grazing near the pool."

Hans went to Blackie and picked up his reins. "Let's take Blackie, so he can get a drink."

While they walked, silence stretched between them like a living thing, but he had to come up with a viable solution. If he tried to talk, it would muddle his thoughts. Maybe they should go see the sheriff. Andrew would know the best way for them to handle it. Hopefully, Constance would agree.

The glen in the middle of the woods looked idyllic, like some place from one of the fairy tales his mother read to him and his brothers and sisters when he was a young boy. Sunlight broke through the branches that arched over the spring-fed pool, making the surface sparkle and glisten. This would be a special place to own, yet the farm stood desolate. What a waste. Hans wondered what would happen to the property if the brothers never returned.

Constance went over to Blaze and talked softly to him while Hans watered Blackie.

"I'll leave Blackie grazing here with Blaze." He led the stallion to a spot in the tall grasses not far from the other horse; then he picked up the shovel that leaned against a boulder beside the pool, hefted it to his shoulder, and started toward the meadow.

"I wish I had another shovel." Constance skipped every few steps to keep up with his long stride.

Hans silently berated himself for not noticing sooner. When he shortened his steps, they walked together. He didn't talk, because he was mulling over all she had told him today.

As they reached the edge of the woods, he stopped and pulled the spade down. "You use this, and I'll use my hands."

She turned her eyes toward his face, and they darkened to a deep brown. "I don't want to make you do that. It's my fault the holes are there in the first place. I can use my hands."

He picked up one of hers and laid it on his palm. Such a tiny, dainty thing. Her fingers barely reached the base of his. "It would take you a long time to fill in even one of the places. I can do it easier."

Hans knew that he should let go of her hand, but it rested against his callused palm, soft and creamy, even after all the work she'd done today. "You take the shovel, Constance."

When he reluctantly dropped her hand, her expression changed to one of disappointment. It mirrored what he felt. "You start here in the shade. I'll go out there in the sun. I'm used to it."

As Hans knelt beside a hole, he glanced back at her. She stood watching him for a moment, then turned to the holes at the bases of the trees. While she scraped the dirt back where it came from, he did the same. He filled a hole, then patted it down, leaving only a little mound that would settle with the next rain.

They worked for a while with just the breeze and forest sounds breaking the silence. Hans felt peaceful accomplishing something for Constance. This was the way a husband and wife would work together. That was what he really wanted, a wife to work alongside him and share everything with. *Lord, You're going to have to help me with this. Did You bring Constance to Browning City because she is the wife I have prayed for?* That new thought made his heart feel lighter.

"Constance." His voice sliced through the meadow like an intruder. "We should go talk to the sheriff when we get back to town."

He glanced at her. She had stopped working and stared at him. "I'm not sure that would be a good thing."

Hans stood up and brushed his hands on his trousers. "It's the only thing to do. Andrew Morton is a friend of mine. He'll give us good advice about all of this."

She stood the shovel up and clasped both her hands around the handle, staring out across the river. "Since I don't have any other ideas, I guess you're right."

Hans could tell that she wasn't completely convinced, but it was a start. *Right, Lord?*

THIRTEEN

Constance hadn't realized just how heavy the burden of the promise had been until she no longer carried it alone. Telling Hans was the smartest thing she had done in a long time. He was an honorable man, wise enough to handle her promise with discretion. Except for the first few minutes when he thought she was telling him that she had come here for the gold, he had been nothing but supportive. And he gave no indication that he thought any less of her father for coming up with the plan to steal the gold. He understood how a man's outlook could be skewed by the circumstances of a war.

She had become used to having Hans around all the time, and now Constance knew that she really didn't want that to change, no matter what she felt before. Now that she understood his concern for her, she welcomed it. No one had ever paid that much attention to her needs, not even her parents.

If things were different, maybe there could be a future for the two of them . . . together. Of course, he didn't think of her that way, but she could imagine them sharing their lives. Hans was the kind of man Constance wanted to marry. A man who knew how to protect a woman. A man who took charge of things with wisdom. A man with blue eyes that could melt the coldness from any heart, especially hers.

While they finished filling in the holes, all she could do was think about the man who worked in the too-warm spring sunlight, cleaning up her mess. Even in that task, he sheltered her by having her do the easier holes in the shade.

"Constance, are you about finished?" Hans stood over her.

How could such a large man move so silently? She hadn't known he was near until he spoke her name. Then the sound of his voice wiped everything out of her mind except the fact that he was so close. Heat made its way up her cheeks. She couldn't remember ever blushing as much as she had since she met this marvelous man.

After giving a final pat with the shovel to the mound of dirt she had scraped together, she stepped back. "That's the last one."

Constance ventured a glance at his face, and his smile almost took her breath away. She turned and started through the woods toward the spring.

He moved beside her, matching his steps to hers. "It'll feel good to get all this dirt off us, won't it?"

She nodded, hoping he was looking at her. She was afraid that if she spoke again, her voice would tremble, and that would never do. The poor man didn't need to be burdened with the fact that she felt more for him than a friend should. Probably, that fact would embarrass him and ruin their wonderful friendship.

They got a drink, washed up, and led the horses over to the water for one last time. Hans thought about the last few minutes. He wasn't sure exactly what had changed between him and Constance, but something had.

He helped her up into Blaze's saddle before he mounted Blackie. "We've agreed to go straight to the sheriff's office. Ja?"

Constance nodded before she looked at him. In the shaded glen, her eyes looked a smoky brown. The green flecks were hardly discernable. For the first time, he really noticed how long her brown lashes were. He wasn't sure he had ever seen any woman with such lashes. Of course, he didn't pay that close of attention to other women's individual features. He cleared his throat and clicked his tongue to start the horse.

Because they rode the horses at a fast clip, they didn't talk on the ride back to town. When they could see Browning City up ahead, Hans eased back on the reins. Constance followed his lead, and they rode into town at an easy walk. Hans hoped Andrew would be in his office and not out somewhere taking care of trouble. He wanted to get this talk over with before Constance changed her mind.

They had almost reached the building that housed the sheriff's office when Andrew came out, placing his hat on his head as he closed the door behind him.

"Wait up, Andrew."

The man peered at them and quirked an eyebrow as they stopped their horses and Hans dismounted. Before he could get Blackie tied to the hitching post, Constance slid to the ground, too.

"What can I do for you?" Andrew stood with his arms crossed, but his star was still visible on his chest.

Hans held Constance's arm as they went

up the steps to the boardwalk. "Do you have time for us to talk?"

The sheriff looked from one to the other, then opened the door and held it for them to enter in front of him. "Miss Miller, please have a seat. I'll see if I can rustle up another chair for you, Hans."

"That's all right. I can stand." He moved over and leaned against the wall, crossing his arms.

Andrew took off his hat, placed it on a hook on the wall, then dropped into the chair behind his desk. "What's this all about?"

Constance glanced back at Hans.

"She has a story to tell you. Then we want your opinion."

Constance turned around and clutched her hands in her lap. She told the story in a fast monotone. Hans knew it was hard for her because she didn't know Andrew very well. He wanted to make it easier on her but understood after what she had told him that she needed to do it herself.

While Constance told the story, she kept her gaze trained on the boards at her feet. She didn't think she could continue if she tried to look at the sheriff. When she finished, she raised her head and ventured a glance. The man just looked thoughtful, not censuring.

After a moment, he stared her straight in the eyes. "That's an interesting story. I've heard rumors about a gold shipment being stolen, but I never heard from anyone who knew for sure that it really happened. A lot of rumors fly around every time someone new comes to town with a tale. I do think that if it happened, the government would have moved earth and heaven to find the gold. Maybe it was stolen, and they did find it. No one knows for sure. If a gold shipment was stolen, and if it never was found, I don't think Jim Mitchell had anything to do with it."

He leaned back in his chair and engulfed his chin with one hand. Constance could hear Hans shuffling behind her. What should they do now?

The sheriff cleared his throat. "The Mitchell family was real close. Those boys loved their parents. If Jim had any gold, I think he would have used some of the money to pay the back taxes on his folks' farm. Mr. Mitchell had been feeling poorly for a few years, and he wasn't able to work his crops enough to keep up. Jim wouldn't have let his father go through all the worry if he'd had a way to prevent it."

Constance gave him a tentative smile. "Thank you for your time."

Andrew stood up and leaned on the desk. "You know, those boys lit out of here right after their parents were buried. I haven't heard from them for quite a while."

She arose from her chair. "A man at the post office told me he heard that both the brothers were killed in a gunfight at Camden Junction. I'd really like to go there and check out their graves before I give up. I did make my father a promise."

"Now, young lady, I understand, but it wouldn't be a very good idea for you to go there alone, and I won't have time to take you for another week, probably." He took his hat back down off the hook. "I'm on my way out to a farm where there's been some trouble. I have to make sure everything's all right, and I don't know how long it'll take."

Hans stepped forward. "If Miss Miller wants to go before you can take her, I'll accompany her."

When they left the sheriff's office, Hans escorted Constance back to the livery, where they left the horses.

"I need to go to the mercantile." Constance turned to leave the stable.

"I'll walk along with you."

Constance would be glad to have him with

her, but she didn't want to take him from something else he needed to do. Hadn't she bothered him enough already? "Don't you need to get back to work?"

"There's nothing that can't wait."

Just as they stepped up on the boardwalk in front of the store, Mary Reeves exited the establishment. "Hans, Constance, how good to see you. I wanted to ask you to come over for dinner if you can."

Hans rented a buggy and went to pick up Constance to take her to the parsonage. Mrs. Barker welcomed him into the parlor of the boardinghouse, then went to tell Constance that he had arrived. He hadn't spent much time in the room, so he ambled around, looking at all the things scattered over various pieces of furniture. His quarters behind the smithy were adequate, but all these doodads did make this room more homey. Maybe he needed a woman's touch. He didn't know any man who would think to put those frilly things on the tables or buy tiny statues to place on top.

He wondered what kind of things Constance would add to a room to make it her own. Would she sew filmy curtains like the ones that framed the front windows? He had cut the backs out of a couple of old shirts with torn sleeves and tacked them over the windows so no one could see in at night.

Footsteps approaching the doorway drew him from his thoughts. He turned to see Constance waiting for him. A smile lit her face, bringing a grin to his. She looked a lot different than she had earlier in the day when her clothes were covered with dust and her hands were grimy. A vision of feminine grace and . . . loveliness in a fluffy dress the color of spring grass. It brought out those green highlights in her eyes. He walked toward her, wanting to take her in his arms and hold her near his heart.

Hans wondered what she would do if he did. Probably scare her spitless. She had let him help her when she needed it, but he was sure that the thought of being more than friends had never entered her mind.

"I brought a buggy so we won't have to walk." He wished he could think of something more intelligent to say to her.

"Thank you, Hans." The musical lilt of her voice caused a flutter deep inside him.

He held out his arm, and she slipped her hand in the crook. When she did, he caught a whiff of the fragrance of spring flowers that wafted from her. This could be a rather long evening while he tried to rein in his emotions.

■ ■ ■ ■

Constance stopped to gather her skirts in her hands so she could step up into the buggy, but Hans caught her from behind with his strong hands on her waist and lifted her as if she were light as a feather. She knew that wasn't true, but the man did make her feel tiny.

While he went around in front of the horses, she arranged her skirts so every edge was inside the buggy. It wouldn't do to have a stray breeze lift them and reveal her ankles or something even higher on her limbs.

The other side of the buggy shifted when he applied his weight. She liked the way the vehicle rocked in rhythm. She could get used to having that in her life.

"It's a lovely evening for a drive, Hans." She kept her gaze trained on the passing scenery.

"Yes, it is." He spoke softly, but it sounded very close.

Constance turned to find his eyes on her instead of the road. She reached into her reticule and pulled out her ivory fan. After unfurling it, she tried to cool her face, which she felt sure was flushed.

Thankfully, the parsonage wasn't far,

because that last interplay made her feel tongue-tied. He must have experienced the same malady, because there was no more conversation.

She thought about climbing down from the buggy while Hans tied the horses to the hitching post. The memory of his hands on her waist stopped her. Constance wanted to feel it at least one more time. She furled her fan and placed it back in her handbag.

When Hans stood by her side of the buggy and looked up into her eyes, the twilight darkened the blue in his to almost black. Or was there another reason his gaze seemed so intense? Once again, he easily lifted her to the ground. For just a moment, she wanted to lean toward him, hoping he would engulf her in his strong arms. She whirled around and started up the walkway toward the porch. He quickly moved in step beside her.

"I'm sure we aren't late." Laughter laced his tone.

"I'm glad you're here."

Constance hadn't noticed Jackson on the porch until he spoke. She smiled at him.

"Now we can eat." He rubbed his stomach. "Delicious smells have been coming from the kitchen for some time."

Mary stepped through the door. "I

thought I heard voices out here. Come on in. Dinner's ready."

As usual, conversation flowed freely throughout the meal, but Constance had a hard time keeping up with it. Her attention wandered often to the man who sat across the table from her.

Hans had a hard time keeping up with the conversation. When he ate at the boarding-house, Constance sat beside him. And the last time they ate a meal with the Reeves, he hadn't admitted to himself just how strong his feelings for her really were. Every time she spoke, he took the opportunity to study her. Since her times out at the Mitchell farm, her creamy skin had taken on a golden hue, and her cheeks were a more healthy pink. She looked vital and alive. Now that she had been totally honest with him, everything about her called to his heart.

At the end of the meal, he couldn't remember a single bite he'd taken. Only the evidence of food having been on his plate assured him that he had eaten.

"Actually, I need to tell the two of you something." Constance gestured toward Jackson and Mary as she spoke.

Jackson leaned back in his chair and gave

her his full attention. "As a pastor or as a friend?"

"Both, I think." Constance stood and started gathering her silverware onto her plate. "I'll help Mary with the dishes; then we can talk."

Mary touched her arm. "No, you won't. The dishes can wait." She stood. "Let's go into the parlor. It will be more comfortable in there."

Even though Constance tried to change Mary's mind, it didn't work.

Once in the other room, Constance sat in a straight-backed chair. Mary and Jackson took places on the sofa, and he placed his arm around his wife. Hans took the chair that matched the one where Constance sat. He wished he were closer to her, so he could give her moral support, but maybe this way was better.

For a few minutes, Constance told them all she had said to him and the sheriff. Jackson and Mary looked intrigued.

"That's some story," Jackson said as soon as she finished. "Do you really think there is gold out there at the farm?"

Constance took a deep breath. "I'm not so sure after what Sheriff Morton said. I think I've done all I can about the gold."

Relief shot through Hans. He had hoped

she wouldn't let the search consume too much of her life. He agreed with Andrew. If the gold really was stolen, he didn't think it was anywhere near Browning City or the Mitchell farm.

Jackson continued to study Constance. "But you're not satisfied with your quest, are you?"

"No." She rubbed her palms together. "I want to be sure that Jim Mitchell is really dead. If he isn't, I need to continue to search for him."

"Didn't you say Andrew would take you sometime next week?" Compassion filled Mary's face and her tone.

"Yes." Constance sounded hesitant. "But I really wanted to go before then."

She gazed at Hans, and he felt her expression travel straight to his heart. He wanted to ease her burden in any way he could.

"I told her I could escort her to Camden Junction, but we have one problem."

"What problem?" Constance sounded surprised.

"Well, it's at least a five-hour journey on horseback. A buggy would take even longer. We couldn't make it there and back in one day."

Constance looked puzzled. Her expression changed the moment she realized what he was getting at. "Oh, even if we had separate rooms at the hotel, it might not look right." Her voice had a catch in it, and she looked discouraged.

Mary gave a soft clap. "I have a wonderful idea. My parents live in Camden Junction. Father is the doctor, and they have a large house. I'm sure they would be glad for Constance to stay with them. I want to send Mother some vegetables from the Community Garden. This would be a good opportunity. I could write Mother a note for you to take with you."

Hans watched Constance's expression while her friend talked. By the time Mary finished, hope had replaced the look of discouragement.

"I think that is a good idea, Constance." When he spoke, she turned a grateful expression toward him. "When would you like to go?"

"I can't go tomorrow because I was gone from the boardinghouse kitchen today." Constance looked thoughtful for a moment. "I could bake double everything tomorrow, and we could go the next day." She smiled at him. "If you aren't too busy, Hans."

He would never get tired of hearing her speak his name. This time it came out softly with great emotion, rendering him speechless.

Just as Mary had said, her parents welcomed Constance into their home with open arms. She would have known Mrs. Carter was Mary's mother without having been told. They looked just alike and more like sisters than mother and daughter.

Even though they arrived mid-afternoon and the Carters weren't expecting them, Mary's mother insisted on feeding them right away. While Hans took care of the horses in the barn behind the house and Constance freshened up in a bedroom on the second story, Mrs. Carter must have been busy. When Constance came down the stairs, a cold feast spread out across the table in the dining room.

A knock sounded on the back door.

"Oh dear, I hope it's not someone coming to take Doc away from us right when we want to get acquainted with Jackson and Mary's friends." Mrs. Carter wiped her hands on a tea towel and stuck the end of it in her apron pocket before opening the door. "Come on in, Mr. Van de Kieft. You didn't have to knock."

"Hans." He still held his hat in his hand. "Please, call me Hans."

Constance watched him from the doorway. She could tell that his smile captivated Mrs. Carter almost as much as it did her.

"Of course, Hans. I hope you're hungry." Mary's mother bustled over to the cabinet and picked up a tray that contained thick slices of ham and some kind of cheese.

The table already held a platter of some kind of bread. It was darker than any Constance had ever made. Maybe Mrs. Carter would give her the recipe before they went back home.

A crock of homemade pickles added a piquant air to the room. A hint of spices, vinegar, and even sweetness. Sliced tomatoes and onions covered another plate. Constance hadn't realized how hungry she was until she looked at all the food.

The doctor returned from his office in the front of the large first floor, and they all sat down to eat. After he blessed their food, Mrs. Carter passed each plate to Constance first, then to Hans. He must have been hungrier than she was, because soon his plate was piled high.

Conversation flowed freely here, just as it did at Jackson and Mary's house. After the Carters asked several questions about their daughter and her husband, they moved on to getting to know Hans and Constance.

When Mrs. Carter found out that all of

Constance's family was gone, she patted Constance's hand. "We'll just have to make you a part of our family."

Constance almost felt like another daughter, filling a void she hadn't known existed in her heart.

At the end of the meal, Hans pushed back his chair. "I think I'll go and see about a room at the hotel."

"A fine meal, my dear." Dr. Carter patted his stomach before turning toward Hans. "You don't have to do that. We have plenty of bedrooms."

Red suffused Hans's cheeks, and he cleared his throat. "Thank you for your kindness, but it would be better for Constance's reputation if I went to the hotel."

Constance widened her eyes. She hadn't thought about where Hans would sleep. The man was amazing — always thinking about her. Her heart fluttered at the thought. If only she was more than a friend to him.

"After you return, Hans" — Constance looked down at her hands — "do you think we could go to the cemetery? I'd like to get that taken care of today."

He nodded and turned to go. "I'll be back soon." He spoke over his shoulder.

Hans hurried in the direction the doctor

had told him. Constance had reacted to his comment about her reputation, but he didn't know why. Would he ever understand women, especially Constance?

After obtaining a room for the night, he went to the sheriff's office. That would be a good place to find out about what had happened.

It wasn't a pretty story. The Mitchell brothers did indeed start sowing wild oats after their parents died. He wondered if that loss was the root cause of their wild living or if the war had affected Jim too much. Whichever it was, both brothers had been buried at the back of the cemetery away from the churchyard. Plain wooden crosses marked the place, and their names had been painted on the crossbars with black paint. Already the letters looked weathered. Sometime soon, they would be completely obliterated. What a waste of two lives.

Hans really didn't want to bring Constance here, but he knew she wouldn't rest easy until she saw the graves for herself. He hoped it would end her need to follow her quest.

He went back to the Carters' house to get Constance. When they returned to the cemetery, she stood for a long time just staring at the plain crosses. Then, to his surprise, she dropped to her knees in the grass beside Jim Mitchell's grave.

She clasped her hands in front of her. "Mr. Mitchell, I'm so sorry my father didn't come to see you sooner. I wish he had. Maybe your life wouldn't have ended like this. He wanted to tell you about your need for God. When he couldn't come because he was too sick, he asked me to tell you. But we both failed. I hope someone else told you about God before you died."

The last few words were so faint that Hans could hardly make them out. Constance stayed in that position for a few moments; then she started to cry. At first, tears made their quiet way down her cheeks, but soon she sniffled and then sobbed. Hans felt as if his heart were breaking. He couldn't leave her there, so he pulled her up and into his arms, cradling her against his chest.

She continued to cry for a long time. All the while, Hans held her tight with one arm and gave her comforting strokes on her back with the other hand. He occasionally murmured what he hoped were comforting words. The rest of the time, he prayed silently for her sorrow and pain to be eased. How he wished he had the right to do more.

FOURTEEN

The next day when Constance and Hans arrived back in Browning City, they went straight to the parsonage. Hans helped her down from the wagon seat and handed her several packages wrapped in brown paper and tied with twine. She started up the walkway, and he picked up the last four bundles left in the back of the wagon.

He caught up with her halfway to the house. "I'll take your carpetbag by the boardinghouse before I return the wagon to the livery."

She smiled up at him. "Thanks. I want to spend a while with Mary if she's not busy."

He nodded. "She'll want you to be there when she opens all these parcels from her mother."

"Yes, she probably will." Constance stepped up on the porch. "I've missed being with Mary. It's been more than four days since we spent any time alone. We have a lot to talk about."

"I'm sure you do." The twinkle in his eyes carried over to the tone of his voice.

Maybe it was time for her to talk to Mary about her feelings for Hans . . . or maybe not. She'd see how the afternoon progressed.

Mary opened the door after Hans knocked. Her eyes widened when she saw all the packages in their arms. "Come in." She stepped back and pulled the door farther open.

"Where do you want us to put these?" Constance smiled at Mary's look of bewilderment.

"What are they?"

"We're not sure. Your mother gave them to us just before we left this morning . . . along with a basket of food for us to eat on the way home. It was enough to feed an army." Constance glanced toward the parlor. "Do you want these in there or on the table in the kitchen?"

Hans stood quietly and listened to the exchange. Constance welcomed his presence but knew she would wait until he was gone before she asked Mary all the questions that were whirling in her brain.

Mary turned back toward the kitchen. "Let's put them on the table. Then we can spread out all the items and see what they are."

Hans dropped the ones he carried beside hers on the shiny wooden surface. "I need to get to the smithy and see if I've missed anyone. If I'm not there, they just tack a note up on the door." He turned toward Constance. "Would you like me to come back and pick you up to go to the boarding-house?"

She smiled at him. "Thank you, Hans, but no. I've ridden more miles than I want to remember in the last few days. The walk will do me good."

Mary went to the door with him, but soon returned. "Let's see what Mother sent. I can hardly wait. Why don't you open some of them while I open the others?"

She sounded like a child at Christmas. Of course, no one Constance knew ever had this many presents at that holiday.

Constance started trying to untie the knot on the bundle closest to her. The knot resisted, and she became frustrated with her efforts.

"Do it like this." Mary pulled the twine around one corner, then off the package.

As the paper from each bundle unfolded, the two women ooed and aahed. Baby gowns, blankets, knitted hats, sweaters, booties, safety pins that people had started using on diapers, and hemmed flannel diapers spread across the table. The last parcel contained a soft cotton nightgown and robe for Mary. Pink embroidered roses clung to vines that climbed all the way up the front of both garments.

Tears sprang to Mary's eyes. "Mother must have started working on these as soon as we let them know that we were going to have a baby."

"They're wonderful." Constance knew that the tiny stitches had taken a lot of work. "Your mother really loves you, and she already loves her grandchild."

After Constance helped Mary take the items up to the bedroom that was being turned into a nursery, the women returned to the kitchen for a cup of tea. Mary asked all about the trip, and Constance gladly told her the many details. They each drank two more cups of tea before they were through discussing the subject.

"You have something else on your mind, don't you?" Mary's perceptive question caught Constance off guard.

"Yes. I want to ask you about a thing that happened the day I went out to the farm, when Hans came and helped me fill in the holes."

Mary set her cup down and gave Constance her full attention. "I can see it's important to you. What happened?"

Constance studied the design worked into the tablecloth before answering, but her thoughts weren't on the pattern. She was trying to formulate the words into a sensible explanation. "Hans didn't find me immediately. He saw the holes and piles of dirt beside them. When I came back from the spring, he stood near the edge of the bluff talking to God."

"That sounds like Hans." Mary nodded. "He likes to seek the Lord about anything that bothers him. So what did he say?"

Constance clasped her hands together on the tabletop. "It's not so much what he said exactly. It's more the way he said things. . . . I know this doesn't make any sense, but I've never heard anyone talk to God that way. His head wasn't bowed, and he sounded just the same as he would talking to Jackson or us."

"That's because he was talking to his best friend . . . Jesus." Mary turned concerned eyes toward her. "Constance, what do you believe about God?"

What a surprising question. No one had ever asked her anything like that. What did she believe about God?

She stared out the window and watched two birds circling around while building a nest in the branches of the tree. One would go down and retrieve some grass; the other went for tiny twigs; then they both returned to the bower. She needed something specific, like the purpose the birds had to provide shelter for their eggs. Instead, her thoughts flew around without landing.

Mary waited patiently, allowing her to gather her scattered thoughts.

"I know that God created the world and all that's in it."

"That's a start." Mary smiled at her. "What else?"

Finally, things started to settle into a pattern. "He loves us, and He sent Jesus to die for our sins. Now they're both in heaven, and when we die, we'll go to be with God. Right?"

Mary picked up her spoon and stirred her cooling tea. "That's right as far as it goes. Have you ever asked Jesus to save you from your sins?"

Constance nodded. "When I was nine years old." She remembered the brush arbor meeting years before. What the evangelist said finally made sense to her. She had asked her mother to walk to the front with her, and everyone had come after the service to welcome her into the family of God.

"Have you studied the Scriptures and grown in your faith since that time?"

Mary's question made her squirm in the chair. "We went to church when we could get there, but the circuit-riding preacher only came maybe once a month. The other Sundays, we had all-day singings with dinner on the grounds. I really like the singings and the fellowship of sharing the meal with neighbors."

Two grooves formed between Mary's brows. "Do you read your Bible and commune with Jesus?"

"I read Mother's Bible until it fell apart." Constance traced the pattern in the tablecloth with her finger to keep from seeing the pity she imagined in Mary's eyes.

"We can take care of that. I'll give you an extra one we have. I think I know what your problem is." Mary sounded decisive.

Constance looked up. "What is my problem?"

"No one has ever told you that you can have a close relationship with Jesus right now, have they?" Her eyes probed deep inside Constance, exposing her heart.

"I'm not sure what that means."

Mary took a moment as if gathering her thoughts, too. "When Jesus went back to heaven, He left his Holy Ghost with us. And He wants to be a part of our everyday lives. He wants to be the Lord of our lives and help us with everything we face. Does that make any sense to you?"

Constance got up and walked over to the window. The bright sunlight and beauty all around reminded her that God loved her through His creation. Could He really want to take part in everything in her life? Didn't He have enough to take care of? How would it change what happened to her?

She turned back to look at Mary. "I think I understand what you're telling me, but how does that work?"

"What happens when you pray now?" Mary's question didn't answer hers.

"Well, I ask God for strength and help, then hope everything will be okay. Many times it isn't."

Mary came to stand beside her. "You talk to Him way up in heaven, you mean?"

Constance nodded. "How do you pray?"

Mary's smile lit the room. "I imagine I pray much like Hans did. Jesus is my friend. He listens to me, and I listen to Him. He really cares about my life."

One thing Mary said caught Constance's attention. "What do you mean, you listen to Him?"

A faraway look came over Mary's face. "Sometimes, He talks to me through Scripture. Other times, He drops thoughts and assurances into my heart. He even speaks to me through Jackson, both as my husband and as my pastor. I have a personal relationship with Him. When you ask Him to direct your life, He will give you peace in your heart. The Bible talks about a peace that passeth understanding. If I'm not certain about whether He wants me to do something, I see if I have a peace about it."

Constance sat back down and took a sip of her stone-cold tea. At least it wet her throat, which was dry from all the talking.

"So how do I do that?"

Mary studied her intently for a moment. "You just pray and ask Him to show you what He wants you to do in every situation and relationship you face. He's a gentleman. He won't force you to involve Him in your daily life and do what He wants."

A gentleman. Maybe that's why Hans was such a gentleman. He tried to treat others as Jesus did. "I'd like that, but I'm not sure exactly what to say or how to say it."

Mary sat down across the table from her and reached to take her hands. "You just talk to Him as you would talk to me. Tell Him what's in your heart. If you want me to, I can say a phrase, and if you agree, you can repeat it."

Finally, Constance didn't feel as if she were wandering through a strange forest without a map or compass. "I'd like that. Should I bow my head?"

"If you want to, but your head doesn't have to be bowed to talk to Him."

Constance decided she wanted to, because she was sure this would be a sacred time. A time she would want to remember forever.

"Jesus, I ask You to lead me through my life."

Constance thought about this sentence, then repeated it.

"I want You to take part in everything I do and show me how You want me to live."

This time Constance repeated the words immediately.

"Thank You for loving me and wanting to have a deeper relationship with me."

These words tumbled from Constance's heart as well as her mouth, and something happened. She could feel the presence of Jesus so strong that it invaded every part of her. Tears became a waterfall down her cheeks. Love filled every part of her heart. More love than she had ever known existed. She bowed silently before the overwhelming presence, basking in Him. All her life, she had wanted this, but she hadn't known exactly what it was that she was looking for.

She wondered why no one had ever told her about it. Maybe someone had, and she hadn't understood what they were talking about.

Constance wanted to share it with everyone in the world, but for right now, she would just spend time with Him, letting Him establish His peace and love in her heart.

When Hans went to the boardinghouse for supper, he could hardly wait to see Constance. Spending most of three days this week with her made him miss her when they were apart. *Lord, what's going on here?*

Mrs. Barker welcomed him to the table, but he didn't see Constance. He glanced toward the doorway to the kitchen as she came through, carrying a large platter of fried chicken. One of his favorites. His stomach gave a loud growl in response to the fragrance that filled the room.

Mrs. Barker cut her eyes toward him and grinned. "So, Hans, did you miss my cooking while you were away?"

"Ja."

He turned his smile toward Constance as she took the seat beside him. Too bad she wasn't across from him as she had been in Camden Junction. Something looked different about her. He couldn't decide what. As usual, wisps of hair that weren't confined into the bun at the base of her neck framed her face. Her eyes were a different thing altogether. They sparkled with an inner light that intensified the golden flecks. Why had he never noticed this before?

Hans had spent a lot of time studying Constance as she sat across from him at the Carters' house. He shouldn't have missed anything this startling.

"So, Constance." He had to clear his throat to dislodge a lump. "Now that you've found out everything you needed to find, will you go home to Arkansas, or will you stay in Iowa?"

She looked up from putting food on her plate and paused with the spoon in her hand. She took a moment to answer. "I really like Browning City."

Good. That's what he wanted to hear.

"Even though I miss the mountains, the view from the bluff over the Mississippi River is almost as good." She put the spoon back in the bowl and passed it to him.

He heaped mashed potatoes on his plate, ready to add the delicious cream gravy that was one of Mrs. Barker's specialties.

"I've made a lot of friends here." Constance glanced around the table at each one there. "More than I had back home."

Hans passed the gravy boat to Thomas and nearly dropped it. Hans wiped his sweaty palms along his pant legs. Paper crinkled in his pocket.

"I forgot." He reached into his front pocket and extracted an envelope. "When I was at the post office, Hiram asked if I would be seeing you this evening. Wanted me to give this to you." He handed the letter to Constance. "Looks like it came from Arkansas."

Constance nodded and stuck the letter in the pocket of her apron.

After supper, he asked if she wanted to go for a walk before it got too dark. She glanced toward her employer and started to shake her head.

"You go ahead, Constance." Mrs. Barker made a shooing motion with both hands. "You did most of supper for me, so I'll do the dishes."

They stepped out into the mellow twilight. A gentle breeze stirred the leaves on the trees, and the chirping of birds settling down on their nests accompanied the symphony of crickets and frogs. Hans always liked this time of evening, and today he would enjoy it even more because he was spending it with Constance.

When they walked down the street in the quiet neighborhood, their shoulders almost touched. He felt her presence beside him as a tangible connection.

"Didn't you want to see what the letter said?" He smiled down at her, thinking that if he had his arm around her, she would fit just right against his side.

"I took a peek when I removed my apron. The Smiths are buying my farm. They'll send all my personal possessions in a crate and the money in a strongbox on the stage."

He walked silently for a few steps, then stopped beneath the branches of a cottonwood tree, facing Constance. "Does that mean that you don't have any ties back there now?"

When she turned her gaze up to connect with his, the new sparkle shone, even in the shadows. "Yes, it does. I'm now a permanent part of Browning City society." She smiled, lighting the whole area around them with the force of it.

That smile warmed Hans all the way through. He could get used to experiencing that feeling. He wondered what she would do if he smoothed his fingers across her cheek. His hand ached to do that very thing.

After he left Constance at the boarding-house, Hans started toward his lonely quarters behind the smithy. It had never seemed that way before Constance came to town. He stopped and stared up at the twinkling lights in the sky. The full moon bathed everything in a glistening glow.

"Lord, something's different about Constance. Does it have anything to do with You?" He waited and listened for the still small voice that whispered a quiet *yes* into his heart. "Is she the woman You created for me? Am I supposed to court her?"

Peace descended deeper inside him, and he felt as though he was on the road that God had laid out for him since the beginning of time. He would court her, but first he had to do one thing.

The next morning after he fixed a quiet breakfast for himself, Hans headed straight to the office of the county tax collector. The man had an office in Browning City.

"What can I do for you, Hans?" William Lawrence stood up from the chair behind a large desk and held out his hand. "All your taxes have been paid."

Hans shook hands and nodded. "Ja, I know. I wanted to check on the Mitchell farm. Andrew said the parents were really behind on their taxes."

Mr. Lawrence clucked his tongue. "It's a sad situation. I had hoped that when the boys returned, they would be able to help their parents. But it didn't happen."

"Are there any other heirs?" Hans hoped not.

"None that we've been able to find." The man sat back down and took a ledger from one of the drawers in his desk. He opened it and ran his finger down the page. "It's scheduled to be in the auction next month, sold for back taxes."

Hans tried not to smile at someone else's difficulty. "Would it be possible for me to pay all the back taxes and redeem the property before the auction?"

Mr. Lawrence rocked in his chair for a moment. "Well, we've never come up against that question before. I don't see why not. All the county wants is the back taxes. Are you sure you want to do that? It's quite a large sum."

"Ja." Hans stuck his hands in the front pockets of his trousers. "I have quite a bit of money saved. I knew I would want to have a house eventually."

The tax collector picked up a pen and wrote on a piece of paper. "If you bring me this amount, I'll make sure the property is deeded to you."

Hans studied the number for a moment. He could handle it. "Okay, you'll have it in the next few days." He folded the paper and put it in his shirt pocket before holding out his hand. "Nice doing business with you."

All the way back to the smithy, Hans whistled and started making plans.

FIFTEEN

Several people came to the smithy on Saturday with work for Hans. He was glad for the business, but some of them needed their things right away, so he had to put his plans on hold. Hans needed a large fire in the forge, which made the June day extremely hot. He wished he could remove his shirt and work without it, but there were too many people in town today. He didn't want to offend any ladies who might come with their husbands to the nearby livery or to the smithy.

Hans laid his tools on the long table beside one wall of the cavernous room, then reached for the bandanna in his back pocket. After wiping the sweat from his brow, he hung the wet cloth across a bar by the door. Good thing he brought extra handkerchiefs today.

He wished he had time to talk to Jackson. His friend could help him decide the best way to approach the next few days. After spending several hours talking to the Lord last night, Hans was convinced that God brought Constance to Browning City for several reasons. The main one was to meet him.

His parents had taught their sons the proper way to court a woman. A man should approach the man who was the protector of the woman and ask his permission first. Constance didn't have a father, brother, or uncle for him to talk to.

When Hans went over in his mind all the times he and Constance had been together, he realized that there was a possibility she already felt something more than friendship for him, but he wasn't sure. How could he bring up the subject to explore their feelings? His ran deep, but he couldn't always put them into words. Maybe Jackson could tell him what to do. Any suggestions would be helpful.

As he returned to shaping a horseshoe against his anvil, every pound of the hammer contained some of his frustration. Rhythmical beats of iron against iron rang through the building and echoed into the street.

"Are you trying to beat that thing to death?" Jackson's laugh followed his question as he came in out of the sun. "It sure is hot in here." He took off his hat and fanned his face and neck.

Hans plunged the finished shoe into the bucket of cool water, and steam hissed in a cloud, adding to the oppressive heat. After a moment, he jerked the piece of shaped metal back out of its bath, shook the water off, and put it in the bucket that held several more. He laid his hammer on the table, then pulled off his apron and placed it beside the tool. After grabbing another bandanna, he headed toward the doorway.

"Let's get out in the breeze for a while. I'm ready for a break." Hans finished wiping his face, hands, and forearms, then hung the cloth beside the first one. "So what brings you by the smithy? Do you need something repaired?"

Jackson shook his head. "No. I just felt that I should come by and see you."

Hans laughed. "You must have been listening to the Lord. I've been bending His ear enough this morning, wishing I could talk to you."

Jackson waved toward a bench that sat in the shade of a giant oak tree across the road. "Do you have time to sit a minute?"

Hans led the way and dropped onto the wooden seat worn smooth from years of use by weary travelers. "I can take a little while."

After sitting beside him and propping one foot on the other leg, Jackson asked, "So why were you telling the Lord that you wanted to talk to me?"

Hans rubbed the toe of his boot in the thick layer of dust in front of them, making lazy circles. "I need some advice."

Jackson waited a moment, probably expecting Hans to continue, but he didn't. "About what?"

"I've developed strong feelings for Constance."

The last thing Hans expected was the laugh that exploded from his friend. It drowned out the rustle of leaves in the branches above, and the birds stopped chirping.

" 'Strong feelings,' huh? Just how strong are these feelings?"

"I'm not going to tell you if you're going to laugh at me." Hans tried to sound offended, but he knew he didn't succeed. "I'm trying to be serious here."

Jackson sobered and draped his arm across his upraised knee. "I'm sorry. I shouldn't have laughed. It just took you long enough to recognize what you're feeling. You do love her, don't you?"

How did Jackson know? Hans had just realized it the other day. "Well . . . ja."

"So what are you going to do about it?" Jackson cut right to the crux of the matter.

What could he do? "I'd really like to court her, see if she cares for me, too."

"I don't think you have to worry about that." Was Jackson a mind reader? A pastor wasn't supposed to take part in that kind of hocus-pocus, was he?

Hans ran a hand around the back of his neck. "I wish she had a father for me to ask. That's what my parents taught me to do. I'm trying to decide how to go about it."

Jackson stared up the street toward the center of town. "Why don't I ask her to move into the parsonage with Mary and me? My wife's getting tired much quicker these days. Constance could help a bit around the house, and she would be under my protection. You could take your time courting her and convincing her that you love her."

Hans wiped his sweaty palms down the legs of his denim trousers. "All right. That sounds like a good idea to me. I've noticed a difference in her attitude toward me lately. She might care something for me already."

Jackson laughed again, then held up his hand. "I'm sorry. It's just funny to me. Mary and I have both known for a long time that you love each other. We were just waiting for you to realize it, too."

"Does everyone in town know?" Hans couldn't have kept the exasperation out of his tone if he had wanted to.

"I doubt it." Jackson set his foot down in the dirt beside his other one. He leaned his forearms on his thighs and clasped his hands. "We just know you better than anyone else does."

Constance had always loved going to church. Probably because of the music and spending time with friends. Today was different. When she walked into the wooden structure with sunlight shining through amber-tinted windows that lit up the whole space, she felt as if she were really going into the Lord's house. God no longer seemed way off up in heaven. Her heart was so full of His love that she didn't think she could contain it.

She slipped into a pew halfway down the center aisle, on the left. After taking her place, she bowed her head and shut her eyes, basking in His presence. Her life had made a drastic turn. Had it only been two days ago? Such a short span in the twenty years of her life. Finally, her heart was full of a deeper love than she had ever imagined.

She wanted to pour it out on everyone she met. To tell them what they were missing by not having a deeper relationship with the Lord.

Constance opened her eyes and glanced around. Mary came through the side door that led back toward Jackson's tiny office. Usually she sat on the front pew, but today, she came back and joined Constance.

"So how are you feeling?" The kind expression in Mary's eyes probed deep into Constance's heart.

"I've never felt so good . . . about everything. I don't think life could be any better."

Mary patted her hand. "Have you heard anything from Selena lately? How is she doing?"

"I'm not sure." Constance did feel some hesitation at the mention of the woman's name. "Mrs. Barker is going out to check on her this afternoon. It's been long enough that she could have healed. Then I would be out of a job."

"That's wonderful." Mary's exuberance surprised Constance. "Jackson and I wanted to ask you something, anyway. Are you coming over to the house for lunch today?"

Constance glanced down at her friend's expanding figure. "I really don't want to make extra work for you."

"You always help when you're there. I like having you around." Mary's last words were almost drowned out by the introduction to a hymn being played enthusiastically on the pump organ.

Constance nodded before she turned toward the front. Just as the song leader told everyone to stand, Hans appeared in the aisle beside her and asked if he could sit with the two women. Constance gladly slid closer to Mary. The only thing that could make her life even better would be if the Lord caused Hans to fall in love with her as she had fallen in love with him. With a secret smile, she joined her alto voice in harmony with his mellow baritone as they sang about God's amazing grace. Today, she understood in a new way what the words to that favorite hymn meant.

After the service, Hans took Constance and Mary to the parsonage in a buggy while Jackson stayed to talk to those who wanted to shake hands with him. By the time he arrived at home, the table was set and most of the food rested in pretty bowls scattered around the large oval.

Hans pulled out a chair for Constance, then took the one on the other side of the table. Once again, he made her feel cared for. If only that care could turn to something deeper. She unfolded her napkin and placed it in her lap while glancing up at the man. He was so handsome and strong, but his greatest strengths were his moral character and love for the Lord. Almost as if he could feel her gaze, he turned his eyes toward her. The warmth of his gaze made her wish a breeze would blow through the open windows to cool her cheeks.

"Let's thank the Lord for our blessings." Jackson extended a hand toward both Hans and Constance while they took hold of Mary's hands, and everyone bowed their heads.

Jackson prayed wonderful prayers, but Constance had a hard time keeping her mind on the words today. If only she had been able to sit in the place across from Jackson, then Hans would be holding her hand. She had felt the strength of those hands when he placed them around her waist to hoist her onto a horse or up into a buggy or wagon. She'd seen the calluses on his palms. Would they feel rough clasped against hers, or would they cause a delicious sensation in her stomach the way his hands on her waist did?

Constance didn't realize that Jackson had finished blessing the food until he and Mary released her hands. She should be ashamed for letting her thoughts wander the way they did during the prayer, but she wasn't. Today, everything was too wonderful for that.

Jackson placed several pieces of roast beef on his plate and passed the platter to Constance. She took some and gave the rest to Mary. It smelled so good, but when her gaze collided with Hans's, her stomach turned over, and she didn't know if she would be able to eat a thing. His eyes compelled hers to continue the connection, and she gladly complied. Jackson had to clear his throat before she noticed he held a bowl of steaming mashed potatoes toward her.

Somehow, Constance got through the meal without spilling anything. She had to keep her peeks at Hans to a minimum to accomplish that.

When Mary finished her last bite, she placed her fork on her plate. "Constance, Jackson and I would like you to move into the parsonage with us."

Constance turned her full attention to her friend. "I might not have a job for long, but I could still live at the boardinghouse. With the amount of money I received for the farm, I can afford it. I could start looking for a house to buy."

For some reason, that statement brought a frown to Hans's face. Why would he care if she bought a house?

"There's more to our idea." Jackson smiled toward his wife. "Mary is getting tired more quickly. I would appreciate it if you could help her. I know you do when you're here, but if you lived here, things would be easier for her."

Constance thought about the idea for a moment. "I really would like being here all the time, and if I helped Mary, it would be almost as though I was paying rent."

"*Ja.*" Hans's enthusiastic agreement surprised Constance. "That would be a good thing."

Mary stood and started gathering dishes to take to the kitchen. "Then it's agreed. Jackson and Hans can help you move your things as soon as Mrs. Barker says Selena is coming back."

Things couldn't have worked any better for Hans. Mrs. Barker had returned with the news that Selena was hoping to return to work right away, so he and Jackson moved Constance to the parsonage on Monday. He had been spending every evening over there for two weeks.

Constance cooked wonderful meals, and

he ate with them. He hoped Mrs. Barker wasn't disappointed to lose one of her regulars for supper. Tonight Constance promised fried chicken. His mouth watered just thinking about the crunchy goodness. Her mashed potatoes and cream gravy were the best he had ever tasted.

Tonight would be special. Just that morning, Hans had heard from the tax collector that everything was in order. He now owned a farm that ran along the bluff above the Mississippi River. Of course, the house needed quite a bit of repairing, but he could go out there on days when he didn't have too much work, and soon it would be restored. He could hardly wait to surprise the woman he loved.

When the meal was over, Constance got up and started toward the kitchen with a load of dishes. As usual, Mary insisted that since Constance did so much during the day, she and Jackson would take care of the washing up. His friends had given him every opportunity to be with Constance. They were almost as excited about his courtship as he was, but he hadn't shared his secret with them.

When Constance accompanied him on this walk through the late June twilight, she seemed a little agitated. He took her hand, hoping she wouldn't pull away. Maybe the connection would calm her.

"Is something the matter, Constance?" Hans stopped beside a field that bloomed with a profusion of multicolored wildflowers on the outskirts of town.

She turned toward him, not letting go of his hand. "I don't feel that I'm being fair to Mary and Jackson. I moved into their home to help her, but every evening she insists that she and Jackson will do the dishes." Her upturned eyes clouded over with concern.

He laughed and took her other hand. "I have a confession to make, Constance. I wanted to court you the way my parents taught me I should, but you weren't living under the protection of your father or other male relative. I talked to Jackson about it, and he suggested that you move in with them."

While he talked, Constance's eyes grew larger. "Court?"

He pulled her closer to him and lowered his face almost to touch hers. "Yes, court. As in, I'm in love with you, and I want to marry you."

"Marry me?" Her voice took on a dreamy quality.

"I'll even kneel before you and propose to

you if you want me to."

She pulled her hands from his and framed his cheeks with them. "Oh, Hans, I have been praying that God would allow you to fall in love with me."

Her face was so close that he couldn't resist. He dropped a feather kiss on her lips. "So will you marry me, Constance?" Even he could hear the husky quality of the question.

Hans slipped his arms around her and pulled her closer. They fit together like a hand in a glove. After waiting for her faint *yes*, he once again touched her lips with his, this time settling his more firmly on hers. Her shy first response set his body to smoldering. Then she matched the fervor of his caress and a bonfire burst forth inside him. All he could think about was the fact that the woman he loved returned his love. They would spend their lives exploring the depth and breadth of what that meant. His caresses lingered as long as he could allow without losing control.

When he pulled back from the embrace, he was glad that they were in a deserted area. However, he knew that if he didn't want to defile her purity before the wedding, they would need to spend most of their time in the company of others.

■ ■ ■ ■

When Hans pulled back from the embrace, Constance felt cool air take his place. She had never imagined the depth of love two people could share. What started as a simple kiss had turned to something much more. Something that could consume her. Being married to this marvelous man promised things she had never imagined. She came to Browning City on a quest for her father, but perhaps the real quest had been from God — to find the man He had created for her.

Epilogue

Hans thought he wanted to get married right away, but Mary and Constance changed his mind when they said it would take them at least a month to plan the wedding. Since Constance didn't have any family left, he thought they would just stand up before Jackson and let him perform a quiet ceremony and not bother with guests.

However, Constance had lived in Browning City long enough to make friends, and the women at the church liked having a reason to celebrate. Every evening when he went to the parsonage for supper, the list of people who were helping the two women had grown.

Maybe their way was best. It would give him time to make the house livable. The first few days, he went out to the farm alone, but soon he let Jackson in on the surprise. To keep the women from knowing what was going on, Jackson came to the smithy each day without telling them where he was going. When Hans finished fixing the things at the smithy that people needed right away, the two men went out to the house. While they worked together, they did a lot of talking about life and marriage. Hans felt he would be a better husband because of his friend's thought-provoking advice.

Mary and Constance went to the mercantile to buy the fabric for her wedding dress. Since Hans complimented her most when she wore green, they chose a watered silk the color of grass in summer.

Constance had always liked the assortment of pretty lace the store carried. They chose a spool in a creamy hue to trim her frock. After they completed the purchases, Mrs. Barker came over to help them sew.

"I miss having you at the boardinghouse." The older woman began to stitch the many panels of the skirt together. "But I'm so happy you and Hans are getting married. I've always thought highly of him. If I had been younger, I might have pursued him myself."

When Constance exclaimed, "I didn't pursue him," the other two women laughed. Then she realized her former employer was teasing her.

"I'm going to have Selena make you a wedding cake." A warm smile spread across Mrs. Barker's face. "They have several kinds of dried fruit at the mercantile. She can make a rich spice cake filled with fruit and nuts."

While they worked, Constance couldn't help wondering about Hans. Before he had asked her to marry him, he sometimes came by the house to see her during the day, but he hadn't since.

"I've noticed that Hans goes out of town almost every day. I've seen him, and sometimes Pastor Jackson, riding in a wagon away from town." Mrs. Barker tied off the end of her thread, then cut it close to the seam, being careful not to snip the delicate fabric.

"Maybe they're helping one of the farmers." Mary got up from her chair and stretched her back. "I can't sit in one position too long. How about if I get us something cool to drink?"

While Mary was in the kitchen, Constance turned toward Mrs. Barker. "Do you know about any houses to rent?"

"I haven't heard of any." The other woman pulled a length of thread from a wooden spool. "Of course you and Hans could live at the boardinghouse if you need to. I'm sure his quarters behind the smithy wouldn't be adequate."

Constance had mentioned to Hans that she wondered where they were going to live, but somehow the subject was changed before he answered. If it was up to her, she really didn't want to start their married life at the hotel or the boardinghouse. She had hoped for a little more privacy. She didn't want to hurt Mrs. Barker's feelings by expressing this desire.

The day before the wedding, two wooden boxes arrived on the stagecoach for Constance. Jackson had been in town when they arrived and brought them home to her. Constance remembered seeing one of the boxes shoved under the bed, but she hadn't thought about it in a long time. Jackson pried the lids off both of them for her, and she and Mary went through the contents. The little cabin in the mountains held meager possessions, and the best of the linens and dishes were in the first crate. The one from under the bed contained a china teapot with hand-painted flowers and matching cups nestled between crushed pieces of old newspapers, along with fancy doilies in a deep ivory shade. The edge of an envelope was visible on one side.

Constance pulled it out and saw her name in her mother's handwriting. She carefully opened the message and tears filled her eyes as she read.

Dear Daughter,
  I met your father back in Virginia and married him even though my parents wanted me to wed a neighbor. When we came to the Ozarks, I brought these things. I want you to have them as a reminder of the life I lived before I fell in love with him. My grandmother brought the tea set from England when she came to marry my grandfather, and she crocheted the doilies while I was growing up. I want you to have something that belonged to my family.

Wherever she and Hans lived, she would place these things in a place of honor. One day, perhaps she could pass them on to their daughter.

The wedding day arrived bright and sunny. Hans had told Mary what he and Jackson had been doing. He asked her to make sure all Constance's belongings were packed. Hans had bought a special trunk for her to use.

The ceremony took place in the church, and the sanctuary was full. More people attended than he had expected, but he was glad for Constance. Since she didn't have a family, she should be surrounded by a host of friends. After the service, they all went to the schoolhouse that was empty for the summer. The women had spread a feast, and a pile of presents filled one table. After they ate the delicious meal, he and Constance took quite awhile opening everything and thanking everyone. It looked to Hans as though they received everything they could possibly need for their new home.

Finally, everything was loaded into the wagon, which also contained the trunk Mary had packed and enough food to feed them for several days. Everyone crowded around, giving them last-minute good wishes. Constance looked so happy it dazzled him. Hans felt almost as if his heart was too full of the love he felt for this beautiful woman, his wife.

He lifted her up onto the bench seat, wishing he could have taken her home in the new buggy he had purchased, but they needed the wagon to transport both her things and the wedding gifts. As they drove away, people continued calling out blessings on their marriage.

When they were out of sight, Hans put his arm around his bride and pulled her close to his side. He glanced down into her lovely face. "I love you, Constance Van de Kieft."

She leaned closer into his embrace. "And I love you, too, Hans."

He pulled on the reins, and the well-trained team slowed to a stop. The kiss at the end of the ceremony had been chaste. Now as his lips met hers, he poured all his suppressed emotions into the depth of the kiss.

When they separated a long time later, he had a hard time catching his breath, and her eyes shimmered with tears. "What's wrong?" He cupped her cheeks with his hands.

She smiled into his eyes. "Nothing's wrong. I'm happier than I have ever been."

With his thumbs, he gently brushed away the moisture from her cheeks. "Then why the tears?"

"They're tears of joy." At her words, he knew he still had a lot to learn about her.

Hans picked up the reins and started the horses. They couldn't get to the house soon enough for him. With one arm, he pulled her back to his side.

"Where are we going, Husband?"

Husband. He liked the sound of that word.

"We're going home."

"What do you mean?" Constance snuggled even closer.

"I have a surprise for you."

She pulled away a little and looked up into his face. "We're headed in the same direction as the Mitchell farm."

"None of the family is left, so I bought it for us. You liked the view from the bluff."

Constance sat up straight and stared at him. "But the house is such a mess."

"It's all right. We can fix it however you want." Hans had to struggle to hide the smile that wanted to burst forth. He could hardly wait to see her reaction to what he and Jackson had accomplished.

When they were close enough to barely see the house, Constance's gaze searched for it. "You cleaned up around the house, and there are two rocking chairs on the porch." Her last word was almost a squeal.

Her hand on his arm tightened. *Wait until you see inside.* He stopped the horses and helped her down from the wagon. They hurried up onto the porch. He opened the door and swept her into his arms to carry her across the threshold.

After Hans set her on her feet, Constance turned in a complete circle. He enjoyed watching the play of emotions across her face as she saw the new floor with a braided rug Mary had given them and all the furniture that filled the room.

She turned toward him. "Oh, Hans, everything is beautiful. I can't believe you did all of this and kept it as a surprise for me. I've never had a home this wonderful."

She stood on tiptoes and pulled his face down toward hers. When their lips met, her kiss swept him away on a rising tide of love.

How thankful he was that Constance had come on her quest. It not only had led her to Iowa, but it had also settled her into his heart and now into the home where they would build a family surrounded by love.

ABOUT THE AUTHOR

Lena Nelson Dooley lives in Texas with her husband, James. They are active in several ministries of their church. She speaks at retreats and conferences. Both she and James are interested in missions and have been on several mission trips. A full-time author and editor, Lena holds a BA in Speech and Drama. She has had several novels published by Heartsong Presents and two novella collections. Visit her Web site at www.LenaNelsonDooley.com.

The employees of Thorndike Press hope you have enjoyed this Large Print book. All our Thorndike, Wheeler, and Kennebec Large Print titles are designed for easy reading, and all our books are made to last. Other Thorndike Press Large Print books are available at your library, through selected bookstores, or directly from us.

For information about titles, please call:
(800) 223-1244

or visit our Web site at:
http://gale.cengage.com/thorndike

To share your comments, please write:
Publisher
Thorndike Press
295 Kennedy Memorial Drive
Waterville, ME 04901